Psalm of the Passing Stranger

A work of fiction, by

Daniel F. L. Endicott

Origins   6
The tempest   20
Holler's   30
Prospecting   40
Remington   48
Covenant   58
Chain reaction   65
A proposition   79
Final plea   89
Vivication   97
The stranger   104

Origins

"Where do I start?" The suggestion of the beginning, returns a humored, "Mine, or the Bowlins?"

Don't misunderstand the laughter: Neither of us finds this humorous – none of it. We laugh because we share the knowledge of a complicated history. Both our histories. We laugh, because we both understand the circumstances and know it usually doesn't end well. But we have you here, because none of us want any harm to come to you – sit: There are some things we need to share. Stay seated until we're through, and I hope, at that point, you'll agree the options are not undesirable.

Please – no: Stay seated. Stay seated where you are.

We're going to share some information. That's why you came here, so let us satisfy that curiosity. We'll share with you what we're able, and then we will explain where things stand. But the first thing we want to emphasize is that we do not want to hurt you.

Unfortunately, you've put us in a difficult position. So, we're going to explain who we are, where you are, and why you should have listened. We've found this usually goes best when we share a little about ourselves – who we are, and where we come from. It was mostly rhetorical when I asked, where do I start, and Remy's answer was that I should begin by alleviating some of your concerns. So let me introduce myself:

My name's Rem Cohen. Doctor Rem Cohen – Remington Cohen. Doctor Remington Cohen. I am a physician, and I specialize in caring for the people in this region. I am a person, just like you're a person. I had parents just like you did. Flesh and blood – just like you – and I make that point so you understand that what you've seen has nothing to do with me. However,

I also want to stress that my promise to the people of this valley is one I will take to my grave: I will not allow anyone to endanger them, and I will use every resource, tool, and all my training to protect them. That's why we warned you; that's why we tried to chase you away, but you didn't listen, so, now – you're going to have to. Because what we say is going to help you understand why you are facing the choices you're going to have to make.

So, sit and listen. You can call me Rem, or, Dr. Cohen – either's fine – but don't call me Remington. That is my name, but it is unlikely that I'll answer, and that's the same with Remy. Rem, Remy, and there is a Remington, but that's an unfortunate story that, maybe, we'll get to later – and, let me clarify:

Remington is not unfortunate. He is a wonderful boy that I have personally taken under my guidance. I'll explain the unfortunate if I get around to it, but I hold the well-being of all Remingtons in the valley with the same conviction as held for the people whose territory you transgressed.

To my knowledge, that's three of us in the immediate area.

But let me get back to how this has come together. How I help the people here, who we are, and how we started to work together.

As I stated, I am a physician. I was a medic in the army for twenty-eight years and after I was honorably discharged, I opened a family practice in the north. There's a lot more to the story than that, but the short is, unlike you, I was lured here from my practice in the city.

Now, you can see Remy shaking his head, but it's a fact. He had some second thoughts and tried to push me away, but the truth of it is that Remy set me up — you did, indeed, Remy.

"I offered a bottle of bourbon."

I walked into my office, and my receptionist said, "Someone left this for you."

I believe it is probably not coincidence that this valley is close to where my life began. I can't say with certainty because Remy isn't always forthcoming with information — all the information, Remy. There's always more than what you tell. But I received this bottle from Holler Stills and of course, I looked it up.

What I found was that it was not far from where I was born, and furthermore, it was near the town from where I'd been receiving calls: A supposed Dr. Schumann had been leaving messages for about a year regarding my parents. Always the same message — I need to take care of them. And every time I called him back, I left a message of my own. It got to the point I just ignored those messages, but then — I got the bottle. It all seemed like too much to be coincidence even though Remy says it was:

"I left the bottle," is admitted, but with a sing-song twang, it's claimed, "But I never called."

Regardless, there were some difficulties that had arisen that were making life unpleasant in the city— yet another story I'll share if I get around to it. So, I — well: I didn't decide. My partners suggested I take a leave and that presented the opportunity to come down here and hope someone affiliated with the distillery knew Dr. Schumann. As I've come to find, no one has ever heard of him.

But that night that I arrived was the first time that I met Remy, and — that — was not coincidence:

"I'd hoped to lure him down here. I hoped he'd like

the bourbon and gain a curiosity. My mother doesn't say a whole lot about my decisions, but she did tell me it wouldn't work. I was happy to report to her, that night – it did. And then Dr. Cohen ruined my glory by asking about some Dr. Schumann."

Dr. Schumann, as far as I can tell, does not actually exist. I have met several people – including a supposed wife that I've never seen again – that claim to know him, but I have never been able to actually speak, nor meet with him. And to complicate things further, the people this man was calling for, are not people I consider to be my parents.

My parents were killed in a training accident when I was in my early twenties. They are why I joined the army and why I studied medicine. They were two of the most wonderful people ever to grace this planet and their loss still devastates me. The people this Dr. Schumann called about are people I risked my life to get away from when I was just a child. They are miserable, cowardly people that do not deserve anyone's concern.

So, as I said, I'm from the region, but it's – sort of – and not this valley. Where I started from is near, and where those people ended up is in the town adjacent – just over the ridge.

That town started as a resort for people in the city that wanted to escape to the stunning view overlooking this valley. You see none of that from here because agreements have been signed to prevent encroachment on this territory, and that includes the view. Consequently, the town is over the ridge and not on it. It is also not where I'm from.

Where I started life is deeper in the hills. There is little to show our existence there remains, as what we lived in could not even be described as a shack: It was an assembly of whatever someone else discarded – boards and fence and whatever else was pulled together into a misshapen square that hardly kept the weather out. The roof was piled with many things, but on the inside, the ceiling was a dingy canvas that sank down in the center.

In the winter, they'd wrap the walls with blankets, and there was a corner where mother cooked where they made a vent, but it was still miserable when it was cold: Freezing cold and filled with smoke. In the summer, the wind blew through, and water dripped and flowed across the floor when it was raining: It was always stifling. It was not a home that was suitable for anyone, much less three children. But the structure itself was far from the worst of that experience. That title is reserved for the people this Dr. Schumann called regarding.

This man and this woman made every woken moment in their presence completely miserable. They were foul and threatening, and the old lady took a joy in beating us until we didn't have the strength to defend ourselves. She'd whip us, she'd hit us, and the old man would dance around laughing like it was the greatest entertainment he'd ever put his eyes upon.

I remember one time, I was trying to protect my brother, and she was toying with us, taunting us over who deserved it next. The old man was having one of his fits, and while he was spinning around, laughing and dancing, his head made contact with the sunken ceiling. Well, I guess it had rained recently, and when he hit it, water started dripping in, and of course – that was our fault. I think that's where I finally realized that it wasn't. That they both were evil and none of us had done anything to deserve what they had done to us. I didn't push back in that moment, but that's the first time I remember really realizing that the three of us did not deserve what they were doing.

When I did finally push back, it was the middle of winter. And I stress – finally – because it felt like it had been forever, however – I was the oldest and I was only six. But it felt like I'd lived an eternity by the time I came home one day, frozen stiff from trying to stay away as long as I could, and I pushed aside the board that served as the entry. As I did so, our dog bolted from the hovel, and the moment I looked up, I knew I was in trouble.

Now, I've touched a little on how they treated the children in the home and I can assure you it does not begin to broach the depths of depravity in which those two engaged. So, you can only imagine how they treated our dog. And that dog not only had the sense to run away, but it also showed me a path that I could follow:

I looked up and saw my mother's eyes gleaming. She had a fry pan in her hand and she was salivating. I knew, as I looked at her, if I did not follow our dog, I was not going to see another day. So, I turned and ran. I said something along the lines of, "I'll find him," I turned, and I fled for cover.

Again, I stress: I was a frail, six-year-old child. Consequently, I still had thoughts that if I found the dog and brought him back they might forgive me. But as the search wore on, and as I became increasingly frozen to the bone, I started harboring a deep resentment. Because just as in that moment where the old man hit his head, I understood that I had done nothing other than attempt to enter the hovel where we lived. I began wondering if it wasn't a set up, and just an excuse for my mother to bring lethal harm.

I believe that's all that kept me going, that night. I searched for our dog, I called his name; I trudged through the snow over the hills. I have no idea how long I was searching when I finally found him, but that dog brought tears to my eyes when I finally saw him: I called, he turned, and that dog sprinted towards me faster than I'd ever seen him run.

I sat there on that cold, miserable night, crying into his fur with my arms around him, and all he did was try pressing closer.

Of course, I understand that the dog was likely cold as well, and it was probable he was seeking warmth. But as a very miserable six-year-old, I took it as comfort and affection. We curled together beneath a tree and spent the night under the stars, together. When I woke, the sun was just rising and I was probably close to the point I never would again.

But the dog was there, and whimpering – cold, and hungry. And the sun was just reaching the top of an eastern hill, and the shadows cast, and the rays of light slipping through the trees to glint against the snow was magical. It was the dawning of the most beautiful day I had ever seen.

I was also starving, frozen, and knew my dog was not doing so well, so I somehow managed to pull myself to my feet and started walking.

I had no idea where I was nor where I was going, but I did understand if we did not get somewhere, we would not be alive for long. I can't tell you how long we walked. I can't tell you how far we walked, but there was some time and distance. And despite hunger, despite the miserable cold, despite feet that were aching from cold and travel, that beautiful morning – the sunlight, the snow blanketing the mountains, and the slight veil of steam rising as the earth was warmed – that was somehow enough to keep us moving, and eventually we came across a road.

There was not significant traffic, but there was traffic. I watched vehicle after vehicle go by as we trudged along the side of the road in snow up to my knees, and I started to wonder why nobody was stopping. I started to anger because if there is a frail child walking beside the highway with an emaciated dog – who would not stop to make sure that they're alright?

I can tell you: I will. I will stop to help anyone stranded, struggling, or in danger. I will volunteer to intervene anywhere I see another that is in need of aid. But no one driving by that day decided to take a moment to see if a helpless child and sickly dog were in need of aid, and with the hunger, cold, and anger that came from far deeper than only passing vehicles, I became enraged.

I began screaming at every car that approached. I yelled, and it was as if I was invisible. I even began to throw anything I could find at the vehicles as they drove by.

I can't tell you if that brought someone to call or if it was only chance, but eventually, an officer approached and I cannot express how thankful I was – I still am – they stopped.

So it's clear, what they came upon was an hysterical child that was likely experiencing delusions – well into hypothermia – and beside was a dog that was in just as poor condition. I was screaming and crying, and my dog was barking incessantly in a manner that I can only reflect upon as indicating suffering.

We were quickly packed into the car, given blankets, and we drove to some dive where we were given food and warm drinks. As that progressed and we began to thaw, the officers began asking questions and it quickly became clear their intent was to get us home.

I remember looking at the man, and – I understand – he had no insight into our experience. But I remember looking at him and realizing I needed to make sure – not only – that I never returned, but that my brother and sister were also rescued from that hellhole.

As I realized we held divergent aims, I began sharing what my parents did to us in the hope it would convince them to take us away. I shared the words they used – which I believed were worse than beatings – and I shared the physical violence and abuse in great detail. I was very disappointed by the initial response.

As that anger that had spurred me, earlier, found new hold as I did not hear the responses I expected – as they tried to dismiss my claims and gain understanding of where I came from: That's when I showed them the lump on my arm – likely a broken bone that hadn't healed correctly.

I still cannot believe that didn't convince them, but it did get them to bring me to their station, and they called in others to evaluate my claims.

That was where the sunshine that I saw that morning began to shine, even when it was out of eyesight. Because, whoever it was I talked to, they took the claims more seriously, and they not only showed concern about my arm, but also, the other markings on my body. Most importantly, they had concern about my siblings.

Now, I've gotten distracted. I was supposed to tell you about myself, and Remy – Remington, maybe – and how we've come to work together in the valley: From the beginning, Remy said, and I went down this road of my experience.

But maybe that's important. Maybe that gives you some idea about why I feel connected here. Why Dr. Schumann's calls were upsetting, and why that bottle of bourbon drew curiosity: All of it's connected to this region.

Myself, Remy; Holler Stills.

Short is, the people I'd spoken to informed the sheriff there was a need to see if the conditions we were living in were as bad as I had claimed. With a clarity I'd never held, prior, I shared the path we'd followed to the freeway, remembering the details of the hills, the frozen creeks, and even some of the trees. I watched as – as a child, it looked like an army – numerous men bundled up, loaded up, and headed off to retrace my journey through the forest.

I like to think the information that I gave them was helpful, but it's likely the footprints of a dog and his boy were the most effective means of tracking back to where we started. Certainly, those that I remained with assured me that everything I'd shared was helpful, and as we slowly warmed and filled our stomachs, sleep became unavoidable. When I woke, it was to a commotion, and the dog was barking and being restrained.

It was the first time I saw my parents – not, parents: The people I began my life with. I saw them as pathetic – small, and worthless. Irrelevant and unworthy of any sympathy whatsoever. They were led away and I was embraced by my sister and brother who were both in tears of relief to finally get away. It was the first time I helped anyone, and I owe everything to that dog for showing me the way.

Obviously, having authorities show up at the pathetic composite we were living in, as well as seeing marking on my siblings, it was determined those people were unfit to be parents. But in those days, at that time – where we were: There was no real infrastructure at that time. This was rural as rural is and social programs were only something found in more urban regions.

I suspect there was some conversation about moving us that direction, but in those days, there was also less formality, and solutions were found where they could be. So – and, Remy: I'm wrapping this up.

"Whatever you need."

I need to explain: This is a very cursory discussion of my experience. We were not well-engaged with others in the region, however, we were not unfamiliar. There were several that knew who we were and that interacted with us on a semi-regular basis. That is, I was not unknown to a number of others in this area. I tell you this to help you understand what followed:

There was a couple in the area that had fostered children in the past. The sheriff – or the others: I don't really know – reached out to them to inquire if they would take three others. That is, three others and a dog. What came out of that discussion is that, considering their ages, they would be willing to work with the younger two, and they'd never had a problem with a dog.

Now, I don't really recall many of my interactions with others at that age and prior. I don't remember anything particularly negative, but my perspective was forged by my family life. From the little that I've heard – and, I have never had interest in revisiting this period of my life – I was a problematic child. And again, I want to re-enforce that this was the first, six-years of my life. But apparently, in those first six years, I had managed to leave an impression.

Therefore, my brother, sister, and my dog went to live on a farm with two outstanding people. If that dog could have talked, it would have told you the same as my brother and sister: It was salvation from the misery we were born in.

They moved to the farm – I stayed with the sheriff for a while.

That time was not particularly memorable. I think I felt some guilt over what had happened. I missed my siblings and certainly my dog. I felt excluded when I believed I should have been rewarded for the actions that I'd taken. But it wasn't a bad time. They were decent and had a son I thought I could model myself on, but I was gone before that could ever happen.

Where my brother and sister went was a typical farm for the area: Decent size, but manageable. They worked the land themselves and only asked their children for incidental help. They had a system, and it was a good place for children to find themselves. At least, children that were not known as problem childs: I still do not believe that was a moniker that should have been hung upon me, and we might possibly get to that, later.

But they were also older. So, I understand if they had concerns and I will never hold an ounce of ill-will against them after the kindness they showed my brother and my sister – even our dog. I came to love them, and I came to know them as my grandparents, as they were instrumental in placing me with the two people that I will always refer to as my parents.

At the time they took my siblings in, both were closing in on sixty. I don't know the whole story of how it came about because I hadn't developed a curiosity in looking back before my parents died when I was twenty-two. But a conversation developed between them and their own.

At the time, their daughter was in the army, as was her husband. They were actively engaged and travelled frequently, and that didn't change after they adopted me. But I believe much of what they'd been involved in was scaled back as a consequence.

We travelled. There were times when one or both were gone, but we more-or-less moved around the globe together, as a family.

I consider that to be the best time of my life.

I was unprepared for the discipline they brought to my life, but that was coupled with encouragement. I was expected to meet their standards, but I was also acknowledged when I made the effort.

I was given affirmation that I'd always longed for, even though I never knew that's what I wanted.

I was given happiness and the embraces of love that I'd never known existed, and the fifteen years I spent with them forged my vision of what the world should look like. I've since found that the ideals and beliefs that they instilled in me – that their parents instilled in my brother and my sister – I've come to understand those values as extraordinarily rare, and I believe they are concentrated in the soil of the farm that is still worked by another of our family. When I lost my parents, when that anchor that I'd come to cling to was ripped away – I was left completely shattered.

It's been more than thirty years and I still have not recovered from that loss.

So, when I say I was lured here, it is within that context: My early years, and then the family I came to love. Our escape from hell, and then – our upbringing in the Cohen family. I got those calls and I ignored them until they aggravated me to a point I boiled over. I called and then I got another as if I never had. I began to call repeatedly, and I never shared a single conversation with the man that claimed to be a Dr. Schumann. And then, I got that bottle that Remy left me.

With the context I've given you, I hope you can understand how – from my perspective – it appears I was set up, or, lured back down here. Even if Remy says I wasn't – I don't believe it.

"Doc – I didn't: I left that bottle – that's all. I'd meant to talk to you. I'd tried to talk to you, but you brushed me off and kept on walking. I thought I'd offer you a sample, and then start talking – that's what I'd planned. But I decided you probably weren't the right one, so I left the bottle. I didn't have a plan – it meant nothing."

If it wasn't Remy, then it was fate. But regardless, if it hadn't been for my experience, for the calls, and finally for the bottle, I never would have come back here. And I should also add – if it hadn't been for Remy. Why don't you share how you ended up being the one to attempt that outreach. Share what led you to become the face of your people.

The tempest

"It was the children," Remy explains:

It was not the first time I had seen a child wither. It was not the first time I had seen the lights grow dim, but it was the first time it had felt so personal – and I know: My mother told me – I should have felt that for every one.

But I was young when I saw the first one perish. It was horrifying, but they weren't well known. At that time, I had accepted what I was told – that we make them comfortable. That we ease their passage back to our Maker. It seemed reasonable and kind to give them comfort as they withered, but then the whispers in the shadows of those gathered started growin' into conversation. Into why, and not understanding why we don't seek intervention.

I had seen several, prior, and it was always sickening. Always the worst feeling to watch these young ones, at the beginning of their lives, fall weakened until they withered.

I suppose… I'd come to accept it, more or less. That there were those that became weakened – that would not survive. That there were some that withered and we should be grateful that we were not among them. But there was always an uncomfortable – guilt, I suppose – that there was something that could be done. That our children were being lost, unnecessarily. I would never have raised that thought to my mother – I did raise thoughts: Initially.

I did question, why. I did question – why do we not if we are able? But I also accepted the response: The risk's too great. There are greater numbers that need to be protected and opening ourselves to the larger world puts our entire population at dire risk. So, I accepted

20

what I was told and didn't press it. But it was always a matter of time before someone I was more familiar with became afflicted – I know everyone: But there are those I know better. Some that are part of a regular conversation. And when that finally happened, it was three of them. All three a common age, and children from considerable conversation. I had a panic the moment I was told.

It was a sickness I couldn't imagine I could hold – like every light is going dark. Like everything held onto was disintegrating and your feet couldn't hold you steady. I started feeling desperate and pressed my mother to do something more, but of course – she wouldn't.

She stood strong, like she always has. She told me I was making it more difficult for everyone – and especially for the children. So, I tried.

I tried to accept it. I tried to recognize it as the Maker's hand, pulling back his children for reasons that I cannot understand. But I never fully understood why the risks outweighed the benefits. I'd always wondered, why not – try? There's got to be someone we can find that we can trust – there's got to be someone.

That conversation got shut down every time I started.

Not only mother: Everyone toed the line – it was one that can't be crossed.

And so, the children withered. The sickness I felt when I first was told only grew worse as they got weaker and it came to feel like I might also wither. I was physically ill and my hands became unsteady. And as the children faded, one after the other, that sickness began to concentrate. It began collecting in the pit of my gut and it turned from sickness into pain. Into a burning that was like a fire that was eating through me. I became so angered that I confronted my mother in front of everyone. The why changed from a question to an accusation, and in front of everyone, I blamed my mother.

Now, Dr. Cohen, you know my mother. You know she is an ironwood tree that will not concede an inch to the fiercest tempest. She will absorb the violence and not flinch while she protects everyone behind her, and just the same, she didn't flinch when I raised my voice against her.

As I staggered towards her. As I blamed her for everything. As I told her it was her fault those children died.

I did notice as I did so that the forest was more silent than it had ever been. I believe the wind came to a complete standstill – I believe the sun summoned the clouds to soften the daylight.

The forest creatures stood statuesque, and the rotation of the Earth was momentarily suspended. That ended at the sound of a crack so powerful that there were earthquakes across the planet.

That ended as my mother shut me down with a hand across my face that left me falling sideways.

I did stumble from the impact. My mother's hand is a steel bludgeon that's been hardened by years of life and labor – by standing as the iron wall against the outside world. But in that moment, that strike only fueled the fire that was eating through me. It only fanned the flames and raised the furnace higher. And not three steps away, I twisted into a rage and sent my own fist back at her.

Her hand against my face was an earthquake that ripped across the landscape, but my fist against her own was a cyclone. It was a war of sky and sea against the land.

I watched my mother fall backwards and there was a moment of unsureness in her. A moment where I had the chance to strike again and take the conversation. However, and – unfortunately – there was also the lifetime of our relationship and the propriety of behavior instilled in our society. Consequently, as I approached her, there were second thoughts, and regrets, and worry for her. As those fell against the fire, the uncertainty disappeared entirely and my mother struck me squarely with her fist.

I think, now, that the loss of surety was merely ruse. That she wanted to disarm me to reel me in, and that's what she did: She clocked me hard and left me scrambled, and she came charging immediately to deliver more.

I believe those gathered were fully behind my mother's position at that time, and there were hands against me that kept me open to her. And, I don't know if it was fear, or anger, or frustration about everything occurring on that day, but as my mother approached, as others held me towards her, my arms reacted as if thinking on their own.

It was inconsequential, really: I reached up and broke a tree branch free. But it was a continuation of defiance. I refused to back from my position: We have the capability to do something; therefore, it is irreconcilable that we don't.

The tree handed me its offering and I raked it at my mother.

I swung wildly and it was largely unsuccessful at anything, however, it added fuel to the fire. It gave me the chance to collect my wits, and I finally used all the anger, and fire, and sorrow that was in me to spike it at her.

Obviously, it was ineffective. She caught the branch and threw it down. But at that point, I'd re-collected, sharpened, and that fury that started all of this was aimed back at her. So, when she charged me – I was ready.

She threw, and I defended. It was mostly backing away, blocking the worst of it, at first. But after a little bit of that – I turned it back: She threw – I threw back. And about that time, my daddy started playing.

He started plucking at the banjo, and at that point, all those gathered to mourn the loss of the little ones formed a circle to enclose us.

My daddy was plucking, dancing, and crowing like Hawling Cratchett as he watched his wife and only son start going at it.

We started – testing: Ma, 'cause she didn't know where I was coming from. Myself because I had no idea what I was facing. So, we danced around and jabbed a bit, until she decided to try and end it.

But I saw it coming.

I was still feeling uncertain. There was the fire – but she's my mother. I had conviction, but so had she. I felt like those surrounding were with her, and not with me. There was little encouragement outside of the strums across the banjo strings.

That's where the burning really fueled again. I heard my daddy singing about a battle. It caught my ear – the struggle to win. The sacrifice and willingness to charge against a devoted adversary. It was at that moment that I had the clarity of understanding, that as long as my mother led the nation, nothing ever going to change. In that moment, I realized I had to take my mother down.

Now, you know my mother. You know this is not a simple proposition – you understand, this is likely foolish: And I recognized that in the moment. I knew I would likely be humiliated and relegated to a place of disregard. But I also could not forget those children's voices, and if that's where I ended up, because if fighting for them meant that's where I ended, then I was more than satisfied to end up there. I never had ambition for anything in particular, anyhow, even though I know my mother had her expectations.

To follow in her footsteps.

To be the face of the nation. The voice of the people. A generational leadership to provide a consistent face to who we are.

And – I don't disagree that could be useful.

I also know there are others with ambitions and I'd been more than happy to follow them. I would have been fine with being a citizen. My mother is a force and I've never felt like I was that. But then these children were taken from me, and I cannot accept that. And the reason why's, there's those out there we know are capable of helping them.

There are those out there that can alleviate the suffering. There are those that can buy time, and if fortunate, there can be recovery. I could not stand to listen to one more excuse why we could not bring someone in the fold to take care of them – to help relieve the withering. So, I stood my ground.

At a point, my father began to really go. He was singing, and plucking, and dancing with an elation that was the opposite of what I was feeling. But it did give energy to the moment. It did rally those that were watching, and they started joining. They started singing, and dancing, and calling out, and it was then that I heard the first words that supported my position, and that fire turned into a vision for a new road.

It was a forcible turn that I knew would change everything if I was successful, and I found a conviction that stood through the pain of my mother's strikes.

The wind rose, and the trees were bending from the violence. Creatures of the forest raised their voices and crowed us on. There was dust flying in the air as our people danced away the poison, bitter sorrow from losing children. It was a salve to the sickness that was in all of us, and the syphon to it was the two of us: Me and my mother.

Trading blows with increasing fierceness, increasing anger – growing hatred: To her I was what she had become to me – my mortal enemy. We chased, and struck, and fought in the cyclone of emotions of those around us – increasingly rowdy. Pain growing into anger – sorrow turning into rage.

We fought in the rain of the songs my father sang with the encouragement of all of those around us. We traded blows and took our punches, though there were just a few that landed fully: Mostly dodged, or blocked, at least partially.

But what had begun as tentative became intentive: Both of us were looking to get a shot. However, both of us defended ourselves enough that it was mostly body blows that landed.

However, over time, both of us began to slow. Both of us tired – arms jelly; legs cotton. We became a shambling battle trying to end it with a final blow, but those were increasingly off target and not as strong as we had grown throughout our battle. Even those that landed without defense fell weak enough they caused little damage. By that point, the damage was caused by our own efforts: Leading to exhaustion.

And, you know, there comes a point you feel like saying that's enough of it. Both us had a point and that's been made. Both gave our best shot and we'd met a stalemate. And as I reached that point, I failed again to recognize that my mother was simply waiting: She knew I'd be there, and was ready to jump the moment she knew I was.

Because, you know, conviction empties at a point. What you fight for gets lost in the battle. You go for a while, and – my daddy's still going. He's still playing, and singing and dancing, and those around us still have the energy I'm lacking. But I was thinking, how do I de-escalate? How do I back down and tell my mother she's right?

I didn't know.

I had no idea how to end the situation, and we're surrounded, music's playing, everyone's calling out, so... I said, "Ma."

I gave myself up.

You know my mother. She played the game until she was at me. She walked up and held her arms apart like she felt some sort of sympathy, or disappointment for where we'd gotten to. She walked up and clocked me harder than any other blow she'd landed.

I won't lie.

My lights were scrambled. I was reeling and trying to find some escape – everything was spinning. I couldn't think straight. I could hardly keep on my feet. But I turned back, and worked for the crowd, and tried to push through. However...

They wouldn't let me.

They turned me back and held me open to my

mother. They forced me to face her and try to defend myself in the scattered state I'd found myself, and all I could hear at that moment was the banjo.

Crazy pluckin'. My daddy going at it like he rarely had – last time the lights were rising. And I don't know if it was that, conviction, desperation, self-preservation, or something other, but as my mother came to finish me, it felt like the world slowed down.

I watched her come at me. I watched as her fist was balled and readied to make the strike. I saw the motion as she raised her arm, and I saw it come at me.

I don't know the time all of that happened, but it seemed like it was extensive. It felt like all of that happened over extended time, though it was likely seconds.

But my mother swung and meant to end the conflict with a single blow. I suspect she expected I was naïve, inexperienced, and probably incapable. And I was all of that and also exhausted, but I did see the blow arriving. I did understand what she was aiming for, and I blocked the shot just enough that it struck my shoulder.

However, she was looking to finish it. She was comin' for the kill, and she followed that shot with another that was less premeditated and more to press a point of impact.

And that's where it turned.

That's where I found the opening.

She took the swing – I saw it coming – and I grabbed her arm.

I had her in my clasp and I saw the surprise come over her. I could see she didn't expect that I could still move that fast. And honestly, I don't know how I did because I was far past the point of complete exhaustion. But I grabbed her arm, sized her up, and then I ended it.

I swung hard and knocked the lights out of her.

I did not appreciate the majesty of the valley, that first evening of my arrival. It was not only because the sun was settling towards the horizon beneath the mask of clouds, and it was not simply the cover of the stormy weather. If there had been sunshine in the middle of the day, I would not have appreciated the valley because my target was Holler Stills.

By the time I had arrived here, I was fully convinced there was a connection between the distillery and Dr. Schumann, and I remain unconvinced that it was all entirely coincidental."

"It was," pleads Remy: "I have never touched a phone. I don't know a Dr. Schumann and I'd never known the people he'd been calling for had children until you got here. He also could have found you just like I did."

It is possible – and we'll leave it at that.

Regardless, when I arrived at the distillery it was with the belief that all of it was connected. That a plan was in place – by someone – to get me down here. At that time, I believed it was to get me to act on behalf of my biological parents, and I believed the answers were tied to Holler Stills. That belief was only bolstered by the peculiar nature of this valley.

Now, my belief at that time was that the name of the distillery reflected its geographical position: At the bottom of a valley beside the stream that runs through it. As I searched images, I believed it was a stretch to claim this region as a holler, as – and as I've mentioned – I come from near this area and my understanding of a holler is it's not so broad, and not so long. But I got it: A play on words. A clever name that did not clarify it was the family name on their website. Fortunately, as I did search for images and view the region, I had an idea of its location, however, even so, I was struck on arrival by the lack of signage. And that harks back to the town over the ridge.

Just as that is out of sight, the only sign you see that references a cross-road is just before you enter the valley: No signs are allowed within the valley as its considered offensive to the native population. And before you ask – no: They are not part of what is generally referred to as the Native American population. Whether they ever were, or, pre-date others' arrival is uncertain. If you ask, they will tell you they've always been here, and there are records, treaties, lore, and agreements to corroborate that.

But my point was, I thought it odd that there was no forewarning to the road that intersects the highway. In fact, if you don't know where Holler's is, you're likely to drive past it. You will see a lot of u-turns if you watch the highway for any amount of time.

However, I had done some prior research as I wondered about the phone calls and the bottle. I wondered if the proprietor thought leaving a bottle for me would be the final impetus to egg my curiosity to investigate further. And, truthfully, it was. That and my partners suggesting I find a place to quietly spend some time until the worst of the anger from the community was worn. Again, that's information we may get into or – we may not.

Regardless, my point was that I had familiarized myself with the valley and distillery before my arrival, but even so, I thought it peculiar that I had not seen any signs pointing to the establishment, nor the only road that I'd observed to cross the highway when viewed by satellite imagery. As I pulled into the lot, I wondered, how is there nothing pointing here, and especially, nothing to point towards the only road that leads out of the valley. At least, that was my understanding from viewing the images of the valley.

There are actually twelve roads. However, only the highway and the one that intersects it by the distillery have been paved. You need good boots, or varying degrees of equipment to traverse the others. Where you won't find roads is the region north of the highway, just past the distillery and the little creek that rolls out of the mountain. A region that is well-marked with specific warnings and an area from which you were repeatedly told to stay away. Unfortunately, you decided to ignore our warnings and arrived at a critical juncture where suspending our operations was likely to cause grievous injury to a child. So, you saw what you saw, and now you're going have to face the consequence.

But we'll get to that when we get to it.

I was saying, my impression of this place, when I arrived, was that it was not significant enough to even warrant a sign. It was rural, which, around here, is ten steps outside of any town or city, so the fact that little settlement's just over the ridge held no sway against my first impression.

As I approached the doors – and I was running, because it was pouring – the thought was in my head that the distillery was a clever way to take advantage of a notably wealthy, if small, community. Of course, that impression was extremely incorrect, and the Hollers' operation has historical references going back to the 1760's.

That's a long time to perfect their recipes, and that

bottle of bourbon speaks to a standard that few in the industry can match. And that, as I'm sure you know, is not even what they hang their hat on.

The Hollers have lived in this valley a long time, and being as they have, they have ties to everyone else that lives here. We will get around to covering those connections, at some point, but needless to say, those warning signs are not directed towards them. They are also, no longer, directed towards myself. But as the signs say, there are severe consequences for entering the territory without an invitation.

We are trying to avoid having you face the worst of those, however – and understand: The worst of those remains an option. This was not a minor infraction, and you were previously made aware of that. Anyone that stops at Holler's is made aware they should not step across the water.

However, Remy's taken over as the face of the Maker's nation and consequently, he's considered the de facto leader. I can assure you, if his mother was still the face, we would not be having this conversation: We would be discussing how to dispose of your remains. So, consider yourself fortunate. Sit back and appreciate that you have already learned more than most people will ever know. There will be a price to pay, but we're trying to help you understand that it is not that bad. This is a new, and more forgiving nation. You also knew what you were doing and went to extreme lengths to conceal your presence, so many of the courtesies they've extended have been ended.

But kindness, and courtesy: If you'd spent time speaking with members of this region, you would have found those are both abundant. Everyone tries to look out for people coming through, and the people here would lay down in the mud to keep your feet clean. That goes for the Maker's nation, as well as the citizens of our country: These are the kindest people I've ever known which does not surprise me, as those encountered are closely connected to the nation. I was made aware of that when I finally entered.

It took a moment to make that move because, as I said, it was storming. The rainfall was significant, and I spent some time considering if I should wait it out, or even come back another day.

But it was the culmination of multiple events and even making the trip was something I questioned right up until that moment. So, I bolted for the door.

I tried pushing it in and then, after a few more seconds of getting drenched, I realized it opened out.

Now, you've seen the place. It's built out of the old mining operation and the building that they used was a part of that. I believe they've built it out from what originally was standing, but they made sure they maintained the pastiche.

I had looked at this building online. I had seen the pictures of the tables, but I did not realize that was on the inside. I watched the rain fall across my vision and obscure what looked like a very old, very weathered building for several minutes. Even the sign looks second rate, at first: A simple board with the name painted on it and illuminated by three lights above. I had low expectations about all of it, until I pulled the door open and stepped inside.

Now – again – you've seen the place. The aesthetic that they went for is outstanding: You walk in and if feels like you've stepped into a courtyard – stone pavers, brick walls with windows, and the plants they have hanging down the walls. With patio furniture and the strings of lights crossing above the space. It feels like you've walked into another world, and that's probably truer for this place than anywhere else it's ever been said.

I walked in, and I was blown away. I stood at the entrance with the doorknob still in my hand and my mouth must have dropped to the floor. I walked in and just stood there dripping, finding it incomprehensible that such a remarkable establishment could be sitting at the bottom of this valley. But it is, and I was shortly, thereafter, introduced to the kindness, and friendliness of the people here.

It wasn't particularly busy, but everyone that's from the area turned to greet me. It was not what I'd expected and I was unprepared to have friendly conversation – I was looking for answers. Consequently, I began making my way towards the bar, trying to keep answers short, and avoid becoming engaged.

But that's impossible, there: I reached the bar and Rally already had a shot poured. He told me to take a seat and he'd get some towels, and he was gone to do that before I had the chance at protest.

He came back and put one across my shoulders, one over my hair, and he set a third one on the counter. Then, he told me to drink that shot he gave me, and now – here's the first big secret we're gonna share with you:

Anyone that asks is told – that's not moonshine. What that remarkable liquid that's been notable in this region for hundreds of years is called, is simply, Holler's. You ask anyone around here for a Holler's, and they will not make the mistake of offering a substitution. There is nothing at all like it anywhere, and the reason for that is, they use a little of the Maker's gift when they distill it. That's been the arrangement with the Nation and the Holler's since their arrival. That is, one of their arrangements.

The Hollers also stand as the first line of protection for the Nation, and they carry that role with intransigent commitment.

As you know.

And I was given the same breakdown you were told: Ask anyone for anything, go anywhere you like, but keep away from the Nation's territory. That is a strict, no-go zone.

Of course, we do understand – accidents happen. I even crossed the creek, one time, and just like you, I was given a friendly reminder. Remy said, "Don't you know?" And I said, "Of course I do," but the terrain was becoming impassible. Unlike you, I heeded what he told me and was more aware of the boundaries going forward. But that's conversation for later.

I was talking about my first night here, and I found avoiding conversation was not only unavoidable, it was no longer desired. Everyone was extremely kind, and sympathetic to my drenching. There was just a friendly conversation through the entire building. And that starts, of course, with Rally.

He could tell there was something more than chance that brought me. He could tell I was looking for something, so he began leading the conversation: Where're you from? Where're you heading? And when I said Holler's, that gained a lot of attention, and then I had to explain the story: Phone calls, bourbon, and Dr. Schumann. Of course, no one had ever heard of a Dr. Schumann, but everyone tried to be helpful: Suggested talking to the sheriff. They suggested speaking with people up in Ridgeville – they even suggested I see my parents, though I don't believe I shared how much I hate the two of them. But there's a nursing home up there, and it was suggested that's where they might be living.

As it turns out, they are.

Rally said, "You came all this way. Why don't you stop by?"

That night, everyone made it seem like a good idea, but when I finally did, I realized it wasn't.

But everything was good, that night. I had a few drinks, had some of their amazing food, and I was fully engaged with the others present. And that's when I first met Remy.

"I walked in, took one look, and thought – nope: It's not gonna be him."

He walked in, and I could tell he was different. There is just this sense of – presence – to him: He's tall and lanky. He's got that wispy beard and hair that looks like silken threads. And, of course, the silver coat that completely wraps him. He appears young, but that night, I knew immediately I would be mistaken to dismiss him: He had an air about him that changed the room.

Some were friendly with him – some were not. I discovered Sheriff Slightman was there that evening, and he would later warn me to avoid him.

Avoid all of them. To mind my business in their presence, and make sure to avoid their property.

He walked in, scanned the room, spoke with a few, and then he looked at me. He said:

"Nice to see ya, doc."

That's what he said. And then, he turned around and left.

Now, at that time, I presumed he was aware of who I was because of everything that happened in the city, and I felt a tremendous amount of disappointment that travelled with me. It turns out that was sort-of true, but I later learned he'd been actively stalking me. As it turned out, Remy was the one that left that bottle of bourbon for me.

"As it turned out, my mother is still better at judging another's character. I thought I'd seen something in you, but when I walked in it was gone."

Your mother's a force, however, as I noted, you carry her same energy, and after you left, conversation turned to you. That's when the sheriff got up and warned me. Rally, on the other hand, couldn't stress enough his appreciation. It left an impression of a people divided, but it's more just those that feel they've been wronged after either they, or someone they know disregarded warnings. The sheriff's feelings stemmed from not knowing the full story, though I don't believe they've changed.

All of that dampened the mood enough that I began to think about departing. Having shared that intention, several offered a spare bed, but I declined and suggested I would get a room in Ridgeville. No sooner than I'd said it, Rally was making the call, and not surprising to anyone but myself – there was no vacancy. So, my first night was spent in the drunk room at the distillery. It seemed like a better option than spending the night in a stranger's home, though I understand, now, they were only being friendly.

After I accepted Rally's offer to spend the night, I walked out to get my bag, and there's that storm cloud that rained on our cheerful conversation: Remy's out in the parking lot having a conversation with several children, including one that stood out for having the only bicycle. That turned out to be Remington, and the rest were Hollers.

But Remy was holding conversation, and it was clear the young children admired him. They were excited to share their experience and observations, and I could see how much they wanted his attention.

I had some thoughts about what the circumstances were that would make him a role-model in their visions, and being where we are and what I'd exited, I did make some assumptions. Which, was not completely unreasonable considering the sheriff's disposition.

But he seemed genuinely interested in what they were sharing with him and the conversation was very positive. I did realize, at that point, there was a dynamic, here, that I did not fully understand. I walked back into the distillery feeling slightly concerned about who you are, and – that still has not changed.

Prospecting

"I still had a lot of concerns of my own."

What Dr. Cohen doesn't appreciate is that I did not know what I was doing. I had no idea how I was supposed to accomplish anything, and that night at Rally's was not the first time I walked away thinking I had probably made a mistake. Like I said, we're fortunate my mother's a better judge of character.

But she wasn't helping me at all, at that time. She was barely talking. After we had it out, she got up and walked away without saying anything.

Now, my intention was never to take on a greater role. All I ever wanted was to bring in help. I wanted to bring someone in that could take care of our children. However, my mother did not see it that way. She viewed our altercation as a fight for leadership and once I'd won, she was more than happy to walk away – and I can't say I blame her for that.

But she wasn't talking to me, back then – not much. I had thought she was angry, though she claims she wasn't, but it took a while to work up courage enough to go and face her, again. Only then, I was looking for conversation: I won the battle, I wanted to move forward with what I fought her for.

So, I walk up while she's working in the forest, and I said, "Ma." She says she wasn't angry but she turned and looked at me like she was, and when she said, "What," all the forest creatures went into hiding – and I wanted to crawl under a shrub and hide as well.

But she kept me frozen in her eyesight until I explained to her, I wanted to get that help. And she said, "Why're you tellin' me?" I tried explaining I wanted to work with her, but that's when she said, "You want to be in charge? Then, you're in charge."

I got a real bad feeling when she said that. That's when I realized, she was throwing it all at me. So, I went with it. I told her I was gonna get someone.

She said, "So, do it."

I asked, "Who do I get?"

And she said, "Whoever you think is right."

Well, how would I know who was right? I asked and she'd just say, "You're in charge, now."

It's not even, like, we're in charge. We talk to outsiders and make sure everything's being taken care of, but we don't march around giving orders. We're the first one to show up if there's a problem – if someone walks across our border. But I don't tell anyone what to do: We just take care of what we have to. That's all.

And the most important thing I had to do was protect our children, so I kept pressing her. I kept asking, "Ma: Where do I find them? How do I know who it is." But she gave me nothing. She said, "You'll know when you see them."

Now, I know she could have been more helpful. She claims I had to learn it for myself, but I do know there are certain things she could have shared that would have helped. But mother is mother, and she'll do things the way she believes they have to happen. So I had to start watching people, to see if there was something different in some of them. And there is: There's lots of differences between humans. I was lost until I saw Dr. Cohen. Then, I knew what I needed to look for. The only problem was, I saw him on the television.

I was down at Rally's, just hangin' around, trying to put my eyes on people to determine who could help us.

Now, I know this is goin' on. I know we've been talkin' and you look uncomfortable. So, if I can get you anything, let me know: How 'bout I get you one? A little Maker's Gift? I hear – no? You're sure? Alright, I guess – it's your decision.

So, I was saying: I was at Rally's. We'd known each other since he was born and we'd always got along very well. So, I was explaining my predicament and throwing ideas out to him on how to get my mother to take this role back. I was telling him about the withering and what had happened, but I did not want to have this role, at that time. I wanted no part of it.

So, we were talking about a lot of things when I saw Dr. Cohen on the television.

And, so you understand – I don't watch television. We do not utilize any of the devices that you're commonly familiar with. So, when I saw Dr. Cohen, I had to get Rally to explain what was going on.

He had to explain it wasn't even local. He had to explain about the trial and why Dr. Cohen was even interviewed.

It's not like we're unaware there's a whole world out there, and it isn't as if we don't know your world's filled with horrors, but the idea he'd been involved with something to do with the murder of a child put me off the second I was told. It was the first time I decided to walk away – that Dr. Cohen wasn't worth pursuing. Besides, I felt like I had a strong feeling of what I had to look for, at that point. Unfortunately, there's not a lot of people that align so well.

So, I kept coming back to Dr. Cohen.

To complicate things further, others had begun to defer to me. When there's an infraction, I get sent to offer warnings.

You've seen how that looks now, and that's how I try to keep things: Friendly, but absolutely serious. I bluntly explained why you should not keep encroaching on our territory, but in the beginning, I just had my mom's approach, and that was – kill anyone that crosses the line. And – that – is specifically a role I didn't want a part of. Unfortunately, sometimes there's no choice, but I did see another way and I feel like it's been just as effective. Ample warnings keep most people away, and most that want to press it get the message when we push back further. Those that don't lead us to this conversation.

Back then, though, I was still figuring things out. I was asking questions, trying to fill a role I didn't want, and still focused on doing something for the children. So, I kept coming back to Dr. Cohen.

I asked my mom, "How would I find this man?"

And, of course, she said, "Figure it out." Absolutely no help whatsoever.

But Rally helped. He helped me read more about the trial, figure out where it was, and he helped me research on his computer. We were able to find where Dr. Cohen worked and even where he lived. So, with that information, I left this valley for the first time in my life, and – I was not prepared.

You hear – city – and you imagine clusters of buildings everywhere. But I had no idea they were so large: The buildings – the city. It was immense, and I was unprepared for how fast everything moved. I was unprepared for how loud it was.

The first time I heard the train, I thought the world was ending. It was so loud, I could only compare it to continuous claps of thunder – I imagined it was like the sound of your bombs exploding. I was fortunate that there was another person near, and she explained to me it was just a train.

Trampling steel rails on an elevated tracks that ran right above the roadway.

I did end up enjoying those. Riding the train is very entertaining, as were the bikes and scooters. I don't care as much for your vehicles because it seems like they're always an inch away from killing someone. But the trains ended up being an excellent way to move around the city, and after I got used to all that, I felt very confident that Dr. Cohen would be agreeable to my proposal.

What I discovered is that Dr. Cohen does not have conversation with people on the street, and he won't talk to you in building hallways.

"Let me – just – break in here: I'm sure you have at least some familiarity with cities. There is always someone asking for money, or trying to sell you something. So, I generally ignore people on the street. And in my practice, I do not speak with patients outside the rooms. I have to be mindful of confidentiality. Furthermore, I had been hounded for several weeks by angry mobs. Consequently, my efforts to push past intrusions was redoubled. Remy thought he'd walk up to me out of the blue and I'd follow him to the valley."

Like I said: I had no idea. My mother was not helpful in the least, and all anyone else suggested was just asking. So, that's what I did.

Now, Dr. Cohen claims not to remember any of this, but on several occasions, I did try to have a conversation. I tried to explain we needed his help, and I stressed – we were losing children. I'd had Rally batch up a special bourbon because, one time, I heard the Dr. mention it. I thought I'd offer to share a glass of it and that would open the door to conversation. However,

Dr. Cohen was only interested in keeping that door shut. Eventually, I decided my second intuition was correct, and I gave up.

I went to his office, one last time, and they said he wasn't in. So, I left the bottle.

When I got back, my mother told me I was stupid. I told her, it would have been nice if she would have mentioned that before I was.

And, as is often the case, I found Rally to be the ear for all my failings. Not only with Dr. Cohen, but word had spread that my mother had stepped back from her role and incursions no longer met immediate execution. That unfortunate misunderstanding was a direct result of my dereliction of duty, of leaving the valley to try and convince the doctor to help us out. So, I focused back on that and reinforced that nothing's changed: Our territory is not part of your country and any intrusion by anyone not invited will meet very stringent pushback, including death. As I began developing how we would do that, I began to feel more comfortable in the role, and then, Rally sent the message: Dr. Cohen's at the distillery.

Despite what he says, that was completely unexpected. I had decided Dr. Cohen was definitely not the person I was looking for. I focused on the Nation and keeping it strong. I put my time in to make sure we remained protected. My plan to help the children was not forgotten, but it moved back behind several other priorities.

I didn't stop looking, and I did find two more that seemed close, but no one aligned better than Dr. Cohen, so I kept looking.

And then, Rally sent the message.

When I walked in, I could not believe my eyes. I

could not believe the man I'd tried to talk to many times was sitting at the bar at Holler's. And I watched him turn – I know people get excited when I walk in, and that's because of who I am. Who I've become. So, I know there's some thoughts I'm there 'cause I want to send a message.

But doc's wrong about this area's divided. I know Coal's got no love for us, but that's his father's fault. And if his father had told him everything, he should be grateful my mother offered an exception. Otherwise, we have no problem with anyone: I won't claim it's everyone, but mostly, people take the Maker's gift. We share it to show our appreciation for the people that live around us, and in return, they do what they can to keep others from intruding. There's very few that live in the valley that have an issue with us.

"Up in Ridgeville, though. There have been several attempts to move deeper into the valley – to build homes that overlook the view they came for."

Well, they won't. And they've discovered that's a federal issue. We gave them the park, and that's more than enough concessions on our end. We were here for hundreds of years and bothered no one, so the least they can do is return that courtesy. No one ever thought it would get as developed as it is.

"There was money. It was bound to draw interest."

You're bound by the agreements that have been written. They're one push away from being moved out of here, entirely.

"Remy: We are on the same page. My point was, simply, there is some pushback in the region. Perhaps elements in Ridgeville, versus the valley, but there are some that take issue with the restrictions, as well as your presence in the valley. Sheriff Slightman is far from the only one."

Coal's a moron.

I hate to say things like that, but he's aware of what happened. He's aware of his father's transgressions, and that my mother would listen to what his own once plead, should give that man only appreciation for our Nation.

If my mother's got a soft spot, it's the love you carry for one another.

I also wouldn't be surprised if Coal also saw you on the television and found out you're from around the area. I wouldn't be surprised at all if he's the person claiming to be Dr. Schumann.

Remington

I do not believe that Sheriff Slightman postured as Dr. Schumann, although Remy's suggestion has also crossed my mind:

In the first few days I spent here, there were several attempts at coercion. I am also aware that the sheriff works closely with the federal government and specifically regarding interactions with the Wasakani, which is a nomination only used by those outside the valley.

"It was something, like, rising lights, in the language of some of the first people to come through here. It got mangled from a couple words, but that's what they used to call us."

I know I don't have to explain to you why that's how they were described.

Back to the Sheriff, though, I was slightly suspicious in the first few days because he did encourage me to engage with them – after first telling me to avoid them entirely. And after word got around I had accepted an invitation to enter their territory, there was a strong push to gather information. It was not long after that I was detained by federal agents for the first time.

However, Dr. Schumann speaks very clearly and professionally. Furthermore, he does not use the regional pronunciations which would make him notable if anybody encountered him. In every message that he left, his voice and pronunciations were consistent. I have recorded the sheriff – and, I am certainly no expert – but I think it is unlikely that Sheriff Slightman could pull off that voice, that consistently. I also asked him and he claims that night at Rally's was the first time he ever saw me.

It is certainly an intriguing thought, especially if

word got out Remy was trying to find me, and – that conversation was not conducted privately. So, it is possible, but at this point I lean towards, it's unlikely.

I also discussed Dr. Schumann with the Sheriff and it seemed like he was attempting to be helpful: He pointed me to offices and the nursing home, as well as some locals that were well-connected. The first I approached was Rally, though I didn't realize that was his home when I first approached.

I will tell you, Rally is not as engaging, nor welcoming outside of the distillery, and that is probably an inherited trait that reflects the family history. Especially when faced by a relative stranger that spent an evening spinning a peculiar story.

Initially, I believed that was just irritation to be bothered at his private residence. However, I have learned – and this continues to strike me as absolutely bizarre – there are several in this area that believe they knew me as a child.

As I shared previously, I do recall conversations regarding my behavior and reputation, but I did not grow up here. I am one-hundred-percent certain they have confused me as someone else: Remington is not an unheard-of name around this region. As I said, there are presently three that I'm aware of in this valley. I was also a malnourished, dirty, little boy that would have been bullied, not calling other people names and starting fights. I think, possibly, this other Remy is why the Cohens didn't want me in their home. I believe they thought I was someone else.

But Rally's convinced. He claims we used to get in fights, and especially regarding Annie – he claims I used to harass her endlessly: Taunting her, pinching her, pushing her down, and calling her vile names.

I do not recall any of that. My memory's imperfect, but I do recall my early days and those were mostly spent in the forest, either by myself or with my brother and my sister. I do not recall many interactions with others, and most that I do remember were with adults. Furthermore, there's no reason we would have interacted. I was not in school, and while I'm from the region, getting to where I started is an hour by car. I do not believe that there is any possibility that we would have interacted, but they don't buy it.

So, I apologized. I told Rally, and I told Annie, if it was me, I've forced it from my memory, and if it was, I told them I was sorry – but it wasn't.

I am not in denial. I do not run away from what I've done, but I did not begin my life in this valley.

Anyway, I got through that with Rally, and like everyone, he pointed to the usual places where a doctor might be working, and like everyone, he suggested if he was living here, he'd be in the gated homes that started the development that became Ridgeville.

At that point, the ideas that I'd developed, that had brought me to the valley began to lose conviction. Believing everything was connected became an unanswered question. Therefore, my certainty that the distillery was related to the phone calls and Dr. Schumann began to falter, and I consequently began exploring.

I began talking with anyone and asking about Dr. Schuman. Of course, not one person knew a Dr. Schuman, so I did visit the clinic, and I did visit the nursing home, and of course: You know the story – not one person either place had ever heard of him. And then, I did something I swore I never would. I inquired at the nursing home.

Regarding Nicie and Boyd Bowlin.

And you know what? You do... They were there – they are there.

They asked if I would like to visit them.

Well, I can tell you, they are still the people I remember, more or less. The old lady's still foul, but arthritis has removed any hint of threat. And the old man is almost a skeleton.

He still laughs like he did. He still finds everything that happened to be hilarious, but he can't remember most of it.

And the old lady – what comes out of her mouth is just because she got so used to saying it. She just spits out insults and foul language but I don't think there is any real thoughts behind it, any longer. It was actually pathetic.

I don't feel sorry for them. They remember what they did. My brother and sister bear scars from – and not just flesh. There are scars down to the soul. So, no, I do not feel one speck of pity – I will never offer them forgiveness – but I also did not feel the hatred for them that I've carried for over half a century. And then, as I was standing, trying to sort out what I was feeling, I observed something that was horrible: I saw pictures on the walls.

Crayon pictures.

As if drawn by a child.

I had a chill go through my body to think that someone had foolishly allowed those people to care for another child. So, I asked them. And both of them... Those two just started laughing. And when I took a closer look I was completely baffled, because the young artist had signed those pictures, Remington.

I can assure you, those are not mine. The only

materials I had for making anything as a child, were sticks, and mud, and whatever I dug up in the forest. I never saw a crayon until I was living with the sheriff.

"I guess you're goin' there."

I suppose, Remy. I don't remember how I started down this road, but I guess it was unavoidable: There are certain things that have to see the sunshine, and Remington's one of them. Nothing that's happened had anything to do with him, but we'll get to that in a little while: I was looking for Dr. Schumann, and I'd struck out. But there was one suggestion mentioned I'd yet to follow up on, and that was because it felt intrusive.

However, by that point, I'd run out of other avenues to pursue. If this man existed and knew the pair, he should have been known by someone in the nursing home.

"You forgot to tell him about Remington. You know – that bike."

I suppose.

I mentioned I saw him that first night. Well, when I went to talk to Rally, I turned around and he was in the distance, watching on his bike. And again, when I went up the hill to inquire at the practice, I found him outside when I exited. Same thing at the nursing home, but he always kept his distance.

I didn't think too much about it. He kept catching me off-guard, but he was not the focus. At this point in the story, however, this is where we get to the unfortunate.

I devised a plan for opening conversation. I gathered my bonafides so I could show I really was a doctor. And I began every conversation, with, "This is going to sound bizarre." I stood at the gate and attempted to hold a conversation with everyone that drove up in a car. Of about twenty, I talked to a half-dozen. Maybe a couple more.

It did begin to feel like I was delving into lunacy.

But the last person that I spoke with thought that a house a block down and on the corner was possibly a doctor's home. I explained the situation with my elderly parents and my concern for their well-being, as well, the lack of communication from this Dr. Schumann. They were kind enough to not only to let me through, but they drove me down the street and dropped me off in the driveway of the home.

This was an exciting moment.

I rang the bell, and I waited. I rang it again, and the door was opened by a woman. I bluntly told her, "I'm looking for Dr. Schuman."

She did not react particularly positively, but she did react. She did suggest I should arrange to meet him at his practice – and, I was just over the top. I was giddy. I spent the next ten minutes explaining to that woman why I was there, and why I was looking for her husband – yes: Mrs. Schumann.

I did not let her get a word in as I chatted like a – I think Remy would say, a caffeinated chipmunk. I shared everything I had experienced and gone through, and when I was done, that woman said, "Would you like to come in and wait for him?"

Yes, I did – let me tell you: Yes, I did.

The Mrs. brought some water and some snacks, and we had a delightful conversation. However, Dr. Schumann never joined us. The woman even tried to call him but got his voicemail. So, she suggested I could leave my number, and that is what I did.

Do you know who I've never heard from?

Correct.

"Dr. Schumann."

Doctor Schumann.

I was ecstatic as I was walking out the door, and as it was opened, that little boy was out there on his bicycle again. I asked, "Who the heck is this child that is following me everywhere?"

And that woman said, "That's our little Remy."

I questioned that, and that woman asked me – she said, "Have you talked to Annie?"

Of course I hadn't. I never knew Annie, like I said. I've started to think the old folks started going senile and mixed things up in everybody's heads. But this woman, this Mrs. Schumann says, "Rem: You need to talk to Annie."

Now, she said that in a manner that I took somewhat offensively as it sounded as if she was implying there was some relationship. So I told her, "I have not ever been to this valley before the prior, several days, and I have not been to the region for more than twenty." I told her, "I have nothing to do with that child."

And that woman said, "Rem." She put a hand on my shoulder and looked up sympathetically and plead, "Be nice to our Remy. He's a good boy." And she said again, "Go talk to Annie."

At this point, you can imagine I'm thinking some things that are not particularly pleasant. At that moment I was developing ideas about the people in the valley and what they were attempting to accomplish – Rally, the sheriff; this Mrs. Schumann. As I was standing there, it felt as if everyone was trying to create a narrative that did not align with reality, trying force me into something. What that was, I had no idea, but I became very concerned with what was happening:

Phone calls. The bourbon. The sheriff. The old folks there, and then some story about Annie. Annie and this Remington.

Now, before I continue, let me make this patently clear: Remington has never done anything to deserve castigation, ridicule, nor untoward opinion. He has been nothing but good child, a good person, and I have taken it as one of my missions to make absolutely certain that child understands that he deserves the world. He is, as that woman said, a good boy. I just don't know how the heck she knew anything about him.

He has a good soul, and he is kind. He is also smart as all get out and that bike in question was his own build: It's got pedals, but it's also got a motor. It caps out at eighty-four and he'd like to take that higher, but I stand with his mother: That's more power than necessary for his purposes.

And that brings us to his mother.

As I told you, there are several that believe they previously knew me, and I do think that has something to do with the pair in the nursing home. But no one can be dissuaded: They insist they remember me from when I was a child, and Annie is one of those, and I've not succeeded in convincing her otherwise.

But I did go out to see her, as she'd been in the conversation for several days, and then the way that Mrs. Schumann invoked her name brought a sense I needed to defend myself. So, I drove out to her place, and, of course, Remington's already there.

That was the first conversation I had with him, and I'm family practice – I see the signs of a child looking for something. Looking for the affirmation that I'd longed for early on. That I finally found when I moved in with the Cohens. So, my mindset was, let's talk to this women and clarify with certainty that I am not his father. Unfortunately – she agreed.

Now, I could spend an exorbitant amount of time sharing the conversation that followed, but the short of it is, she did – indeed – believe I was – she does believe – I was her tormenter in the first few years of her life. I explained I was gone from where I lived at six, and I've got documents that can show it.

She said, she doesn't recall how long that part of her experience lasted.

This is a point of contention with several in the valley, but I discovered, during the conversation, that the hostility I encountered with Rally, and the oddity of conversation I found with others was not actually because of who I am. I discovered, it was because of my father.

I discovered that Rally and Annie have a difficult relationship that sometimes has been intimate, and sometimes she's made unfortunate decisions.

After she admitted I had nothing to do with Remington, I'd asked, "Then, why'd you name him that."

She gave another answer that was entirely illogical. She said, "You're the only one that escaped the valley and became successful."

Now, we've been over this.

Furthermore, I do not come from this valley. Additionally, Rally is exceptionally successful.

I was not born here, and I was raised elsewhere from the beginning. By six years old I was moved into a formal community, and by seven, I was moving around the globe.

I tried to press this point, and that led to the unfortunate that I've mentioned. I said, "Annie: I am not that child's father."

And she agreed. She said, "No, but your father is."

"If you will excuse me, I need to take a break."

Of course, doctor.

I don't often share this, but Dr. Cohen's become one of my closest friends.

It's sort of amusing, thinkin' back. Thinkin' of that first time I saw him on the television. I saw him, and I could immediately tell – he was different. Not, like, unusual for a human, but I could tell he aligned.

But then – I told you already: I began to have my doubts. I started to wonder if I could really trust him, and the more I looked into who he was and – why – he's on the television. Well, let me tell you: I decided I needed to keep looking.

And then, I get Rally's message.

Well, I went and looked at him again, and seeing him here in person, seeing all of him, there's no question he had the qualities.

But the man also had a towel around his neck, and there was something that struck me as just a little off. His demeanor – he was not the settled person you've heard talk. And then, later, Rally says he was talking with Coal Slightman. But I heard why he was there and decided I'd keep an eye on him.

That convinced me he was definitely the wrong person.

Dr. Cohen was obsessed with finding this other doctor. He was interrupting people on the street, invading the privacy of their homes, he even went and grilled his parents – who he won't call that, because he says he hates them. Now, I've come to understand his position, but at that time, all of it made me feel like he wasn't all together. Especially after Remington told me he's standing at the gate over the ridge and shouting at the people just trying to get through it. I was like, these people are just trying to get home. I was like, everyone for two-hundred miles knows you're looking for Dr. Schumann. If he existed and came from around here, someone would have helped him find you.

I mean, not you: I meant they'd have gotten him in touch with Dr. Cohen.

Anyway, I got over there and Remington's filling me in on what he's heard. And, you know, it's more of the same: More Schumann, hates his parents, and bottle of bourbon. Which, of course, that was my fault. But it was just such an obsession that I became convinced I didn't want to deal with him. Honestly, I don't think anybody did after about a week of it.

And then, of course – it got worse.

I'd lost interest, so I was out of ear for the last part of his conversation with the lady, but he goes flying out of that community. He goes racing out to see Annie – and I stood there and watched that one. And Remington's sitting there, and the doctor's just losing it.

I understand a lot more, now. I understand the issue he still holds with his parents, and they deserve it. I also know he's tellin' the truth: He's not from around here – I told him, "Show me," and he did.

Dr. Cohen did not grow up in this valley, however, somewhere along the way his parents made their way, and his father, did – ya know – with Annie.

Now, I don't judge anyone. But why she didn't accept Rally's offer, I do not understand. He's proposed to that woman more times than it's rained – even after the boy was born. But she just won't. She stays up in the hills all by herself – of course – now, with Remy.

Remington.

I still call him Remy. He's at that age where you all try to make sense of yourselves, so a while back, he asked to be called Remington. At the moment, that helps distinguish the three of us.

But going back to that conversation over at Annie's: Dr. Cohen was absolutely losing it. That man was upset, ticked off, and disbelieving. He was, like, "Why? How?" He asked her, "You don't find him disgusting?"

The truth is, none of us did. We never knew they had three children that got taken away. It was always just – Ma – and her cooking, and – Pa – who often joined my own with his banjo and serenading. The truth is, we just thought they were kindly old people. And that thing with Annie? I know Rally took a beating, but there's lots of folks that would've:

Boyd was a force of joy in the valley. He was always cracking jokes, and laughing, and the way he talks, itself is entertaining. None of us had any clue what sort of demented things he did to those children. But people are sick, you know? People do things you never would expect, and then they turn around and smile like they're your friend. He was just an entertaining, old man, and she was always very stern, but she was always giving.

She would give away baked goods on a regular basis. And – now, it's concerning – she'd watch kids when parents had to work or wanted time away from them. As far as I know, nothing inappropriate ever happened to any of the children of the valley.

So, this was all a shock for us – hearing him saying this in front of Remington, to Annie.

And he was heated.

Now, there'd always been a sort of uncomfortable conversation about what happened. Everyone knew how Rally felt about her and we knew he got trampled with what came out of it. But he also decided to get over it, and so did everyone.

I guess that sort of tarnished them a little bit, but they treated that boy wonderfully. If that old lady could forgive her husband and treat that child like a grandson, then nobody had any right to hold anything over him.

So then, we had Dr. Cohen losing it.

He brought it down to Rally's and started airing some of it, and fortunately Rally intervened – he shut him down. And that's the first time I had a conversation with the doctor: I told him, he better shut it down or I was going to, because that child did not deserve to have his existence tarnished.

I can't say he took that particularly well, but I did impress: I will do anything, anyhow to protect that child.

I suppose, I probably brought the lights dark as I explained it. I probably made every other sound disappear so he would hear it clearly. I definitely got his attention, and then – well: He began sharing his experience – and there's where I understood the anger driving him.

He shared quite a lot, in fact. He told me quite a bit of his experience, and that's where I first saw how deeply he was hurting. He wasn't a lunatic, or obsessed – he was a person that was offended down to the last particle of his body, that someone was asking him to care for two people that had been monsters – to him and his younger siblings.

That's a term that's often put on us, you know. Some people call us that, or vampires, or something else ridiculous. And I won't claim my hands are clean, but the reasons why are righteous: To protect the land – my people. But as long as the Maker lets me walk the forest, I will never understand how a person does those things to their own child. To any child – but even more, to one they're supposed to care for. So, that night, both of us walked away with a lot more understanding. Dr. Cohen understood certain things should not be spoken, and I understand he's far more complicated than I expected.

And, I also walked away from him: I'd decided, he would not be the one to work with. He was aligned, but that night, I also saw him scrambled, so I decided that was the end of it. Of course, it wasn't, but that's his fault.

Just like you and everybody else, we ask that people respect our sovereign territory. And, just like you, some people have a hard time listening. Despite the extreme measures we've taken to keep people crossing into our territory, there are still those that decide they're going to.

Yourself, that sour sheriff's father, and the doctor.

The first time, I said, "Dr. Cohen. Is there something wrong with your eyes?" Because he'd walked across the stream, right by a sign.

"I was hiking. There is a point where the terrain becomes difficult, so I stepped across the stream to follow an easier path. I didn't realize they were so intractable, nor did I realize that Remy pops up as much as Remington."

Only making a point, Dr. Cohen. We had a very nice conversation, and he walked on – just like you did, that first time.

And just like you, the doctor did it again. Same as you, it was a lot less friendly and I pointed out the laws of your land do not apply within our territory. Both of you assured me I didn't need to worry, but then I had to, because you both walked on our land again – Dr. Cohen at the same spot I first caught him.

"I thought the odds of someone being there again were in my favor. It's a beautiful path, and I was back on the other side before I thought he'd gotten there."

Dr. Cohen was incorrect, and unfortunately it drew my mother – still questioning my strategies and leadership. Well, she took one look at Dr. Cohen, and said, "This is him?"

We'd been having that conversation. I'd battled her to get someone. She took one look and saw what I had, and there was a child withering.

I told Dr. Cohen, "Go on. Hike on, and don't accept any invitation onto this property."

However, we'd been having that conversation. My mother saw I'd brought him here, so, she started questioning. And when she finds out he's a doctor – that's where she offered the invitation.

Now, this was not with the hope he'd save the child, though, he did. Her invitation was intended to make a point – that what I'm attempting is completely foolish. That I will endanger everyone by inviting outsiders. So, she invited him.

I tried to warn him. I tried to tell him to walk the other way, but she lured him with thought to the child.

"I was operating under the presumption it would be a typical intervention. I had gained some understanding of the people. An odd community living in the forest with extremely strict, territorial enforcement. At the time, I viewed it as something like a cult, or commune. I expected they were concerned for an ailing child. So, I said, why wouldn't I try to help?"

He accepted the invitation.

It went alright. He figured it out. And I discovered my mother was actually receptive – everyone was ecstatic: He actually helped the child.

But I remembered the scrambled, and it wasn't the last time that I'd seen it. So, in a complete switch of our positions, my mother's arguing to keep him, and I'm telling her we have to bury him. I told her, this is a man who let someone who murdered an innocent child walk away.

She told me, "There's more to the story," even though she didn't really know that at the time. She claims she could tell that by the way the lights were moving, but I think she's just glad that she was right.

Chain reaction

"I did not mean to say that. I apologize, Dr. Cohen. I did not mean to go that far, but I was talking. You know – mother says I talk too much. I am sorry I shared that much information."

No, Remy – you're fine. We've been dancing around the subject and, while I don't know that it's really pertinent to the present, it certainly played a significant role in how I got here. You do need to be mindful of what you say, but in this context, I feel as if we were heading that direction: Why I was asked to leave my practice.

And that is what they asked – that I leave. My partners were through with all the drama and suggested it was time I made an exit.

So, you heard what he said, and there's a lot of people that view it in that manner: I let a man that cold-blooded killed a child walk away. As a consequence of that, there were continual protests at our practice, and I met harassment anywhere I went throughout the city.

But it's not so simple. I've got an entire lifetime of experiences and I've met moments where decisions had to be made before you could even think about the options. That's where I saw it for the man that people say I let walk from the murder charge. And I suspect that some of what I'm going to say – you've already heard. Because, like Remy shared, I was on the television – even down here.

I should never have been a part of any of it. I saw the story, and I was horrified like everyone. But I also recognized there were several in the story that made mistakes. Regardless, when I heard the report, I only thought everything that developed was horrible. It was also clear from the beginning that some narratives were not fitting as authorities tried to fit them. But I never, not in a million years, ever thought I'd become the villain of the story – I was removed. I had nothing to do with it, and it was just another one of many that left me asking how it could happen. Unfortunately, I got tied in and blamed for the man's exoneration. But it wasn't so simple.

The whole thing started with a fight that broke out at a high school in the city where I was living. It started in the school and spilled out into the street after teachers, and administrators tried to settle tempers. And once out in open air, there were apparently several that took a side and the violence escalated into a major altercation. At that point, school officials called for help.

It was shortly after, that what had been mostly verbal, some pushing, some shoving, broke into a brawl. They estimate that more than a hundred were involved. And as this altercation was escalating – police on the way: Gun shots rang out.

Now, this is where everything goes sideways, and I can tell you this, because I was fed the details down to broken pavement. But there's gunshots, children start running, and there's parents there, trying to assess what's going on and trying to find their children. There's a lot of panic and people are doing anything they can to protect their precious children. And one of the parents – she testified and said she also panicked – she opened the door to her car, stepped up, and began scanning for her child.

As she did this, another boy pushed her aside, jumped in her car, and fled.

This was as the police arrived: They get there, and they see a woman screaming, and she's telling them,

"He took my car." She's pointing down the street, and the police reacted like they're trained with an active shooter – they followed him.

They chased the car from the scene with siren's blaring. The boy driving can barely control the car and hits several vehicles and lamp posts as he's going through the city. At a point, he lost control and drove into a liquor store, and that's where we are met by tragedy.

The boy's panicking, and that can be seen from surveillance video. He crashes in, jumps out and sees there's several people injured – some severely. At that point, the first officer arrives on the scene and he enters as is protocol: There's an active shooter – have your weapon ready.

The officer ran in, sees the boy, and says, "Don't move. Put your hands in the air."

It's four seconds. That's how long it took for everything that happened.

The officer entered, gives his order, and the boy turned. He reached back in the car and put his hand on something. As he turned back around – and again, this is seconds. It is not enough time for anyone at that scene to make sense of what's happening. But the boy turned around, and the officer started firing.

Now, the initial reports were favorable to first responders. They painted them as heroic and for saving several lives – and it's true: If they had not arrived on the scene at the high school, the violence would likely have been worse. Likewise, they immediately came to the aid of those in the liquor store that were injured, and that included the boy: They made serious efforts to resuscitate him. Unfortunately, the officer's aim was deadly accurate.

This was already bad enough, but it gets worse: After initial reports, the narrative took a hard sideways. The boy's face got shared across social media, and his mother devastation led to questions: This was not a hardened criminal. He was a happy child that was loved by his large, extended family, and he had a very large social circle. That woman's agony, as she was on her knees incapable of registering the unimaginable is an image that is impossible to remove from memory. And then it came out, the object in that child's hand was a water bottle.

Let me tell you, I was disgusted as anyone. I thought, how do we just enter a scene and start firing.

During testimony, his mother said the boy was notorious for losing his water bottles, and she'd admonished him on many occasions not to lose another.

The boy was in a state of panic and fear, and it was suggested that the last thought that went through his head was not to disappoint his mother: He knew he was in trouble, and he reached back to get the water bottle before he was arrested and taken to jail.

I apologize for all the sighs. I've been brought into this story deeper than I ever expected. I've heard how wonderful a person he was, how talented, and how well he did in school. I've heard from his family, his friends, and dozens that knew him in the community. There is no question, he was a good person with a ton of potential in the future. However, he also stole a car.

He stole a vehicle and led police on a brief and uncontrolled chase in the city. He lost control and brought serious injuries to multiple people. However, we have to remember how this started — there was gunfire. Many people were panicking. It was suggested that's what he did, and he was trying to get away — trying to save his life. There were some that claimed that he was targeted.

To be clear, I do believe that child made mistakes. However, the boy was thirteen years old, new to the school and experiencing a situation that he had never encountered, prior.

I have been there. I have faced situations on numerous occasions where I had to act before I had the chance to think — and the pull to run from what you're looking at is extraordinarily strong.

I've run, and I've pulled the trigger. On almost all of those occasions I feel I made the right decision, though there is one I'm not getting into where I wish I'd acted differently, in hindsight. But that's the thing: In those situations, you don't have the time to think — you just react.

That was — sort of — where I was at with that incident. But then videos started popping up, and it seemed like — maybe — lethal action wasn't necessary: It looked like the boy had a water bottle. And his family was unrelenting — organizing protests and pulling national media in. And that's why Remy saw me on the television.

Eventually, it was decided charges would be brought against the officer, and I do feel like that was the right decision. From the moment that was announced, I agreed that what happened deserved a deeper investigation. I just never would have imagined I'd be brought into it. But I got a notification I had a certified letter in the mail, and my mind immediately imagined it was a summons.

And, that's exactly what it was: A jury summons.

I think we've mentioned, I served in the army for

many years. My parents were army, and I followed in their footsteps. They were medics in the army, and so was I. My parents – the Cohens – were my idols and made me the person that I am. Who that is, is someone that the defense found interesting, but I have no scars on my record – only accommodations – and I'm also a physician. The prosecutors, also, did not take issue with me as a juror. I was, consequently, brought into the jury pool.

Like everyone, I did not want to be a part of it, and I tried to be completely open about who I am and my experiences.

I don't know if you've ever been part of something like that, but it is not a – maybe this guy, maybe that guy. The initial interview is only an initial screening. There was about two-dozen of us, and over the following, several weeks, we were brought in for detailed interrogation. They drilled down into life events and how those had affected us, and one that they concentrated on was the death of my parents. We spent several days repeatedly returning to their loss, and it was brutal and unnecessarily cruel.

The official statement was my parents were lost in a helicopter crash while training. However, not one person that's claimed that said it with conviction because it isn't true: My parents were on a mission where something went very wrong. As I have been, as well, they were often involved in actions for which there is no record. I do know they died serving their country, and the time of service claimed was not the reason they were given that recognition.

I had been in the army four years, at that point, and I'd planned to continue, just like my parents. And, I did. I remained in the army for decades, however, there were also times I pressed the point with regards to what happened with my parents. There were times I lost my temper and became physical with those that wanted to deny what I know is true.

And that was not only when I was younger. I developed – what Remy calls scrambled – I expressed my emotions with fits of rage. This was something that developed from the dichotomy of serving, while feeling myself and my parents had been betrayed. I felt someone had not done their due diligence, and for that my parents paid.

I paid.

I was not able to put my loss into perspective, nor to work through my emotions and that took a toll on myself and the people that I lived and worked with. I was a good soldier, but I was not good when I had time to think. The more time I had, the worse I would get.

I lost my parents, and then I lost myself. I lost my fiancé, and I ruined many friendships. I got promotions, but I believe many of those were to move me away: Acknowledge my performance was exemplary but move me off to be someone else's problem. All of that got brought up and combed over in excessive detail during this interrogation, and it took me deeper than I'd been in years.

I began to drink, again – I started drinking heavily, again – and while I was living the darkest days I'd ever lived, I also believed I'd removed myself from the list of candidates for that trial.

To verify that's the case, what you do is call the night before, and – and, I was already hammered – to my surprise, I was ordered to report.

That was a jolt to my system.

I called back, again, about fifteen minutes later to

verify and was told the same thing.

So, I go down to the courthouse in the morning, and there's eighteen of us called in, which seems excessive, but I've never been through anything like that before. But being called brought me out of my head again, and back to the narrative of the child that was killed, and that brought me back to ground. So, I was trying to be decent; trying to be respectful of everyone.

Now, I am who I am: I missed the chance to have a mid-life crisis, but I am still extraordinarily fit. I carry myself with confidence, my head is up, and my eyes are open. I was an army captain, medic, and I moved on to my own, private practice – a partnership, but I was an equal owner. I have been in combat, faced difficult circumstances, and had to perform emergency treatment in the field while under fire. I have served my country, and I've been successful, and with those bonafides shared, I was chosen to lead the jury.

The two weeks that followed, we were sequestered in a hotel. We were on lockdown – no television, no radio; no phones. If there was an emergency and we had to take or make a call, a court employee was on the line to monitor the conversation. We had nothing but each other for two weeks. So – we talked.

We talked about a lot of things – family, experience – but we mostly talked about the trial, and it was absolutely awful.

For the better part of two weeks we heard testimony from that boy's family, friends, and others in the community. There were tears from everyone, and especially when his mother took the stand: It was horrifying. That woman's soul has been shattered – she could scarcely push the words to answer questions. I have never been through anything so grueling, and it was even more their words than the gruesome videos.

And – let me explain: We don't know what's happening in the world. There's eighteen of us that have nothing to do but sit at this trial, eat and sleep. During this time, all of us became friendly. We got together every night, shared dinner, had drinks, and discussed our thoughts on what we'd heard and seen that day. So, inside this very restricted space, all of us used each other as sounding boards. People cried in each other's arms. We shared our fears, our thoughts, and our deep sympathy for the family. However, outside of that hotel, there was incredible anger.

Videos were circulated that appeared to show the officer firing as he entered – but you have to remember: There was a gaping hole in that building. That officer was watching that scene unfold before he entered. But it was emotional. The boy was an unquestionably good child. He was loved by so many, and his mother was left so incredibly heartbroken.

The last two days, the defense explained circumstances from their perspective. They were described as clinical and unconvincing.

However, I told you I've been there. I have been in situations where you act before you think, so when she explained, the officer had been led to believe he was chasing the active shooter. As he approached, he saw people on the ground and the boy had reached for something. At that moment, the officer just reacted.

Now, we watched that poor child's execution so many times, from so many angles that it will haunt me for eternity. In all but the officer's own, the boy clearly has a bottle.

Defense shares their perspective, and then they give

it to us to make a decision.

I do believe they were hanging their hat on an appeal, because the consensus in the city, in the media, was that the prosecutor nailed it.

However, that opinion was mostly gained with emotion, and in my opinion – that was a mistake. I heard the explanation of the defense – and that made sense. I know what it feels like to think your life is going to end. I know you're not going to wait to see what's in his hand. I know – I would have done the same thing. So, I could not vote to convict that officer of murder, and, I was the only one.

Over several days, I did manage to get two others to understand that perspective, but that was it. The majority saw what the general public did: A good boy in a panic trying to save his life, and in the midst of that, he was doing what his mother said – remembering his bottle.

You can understand, there is no way of fixing what happened. But it is equally tragic to put a man that followed training to the letter into prison.

I will tell you, what had felt like it might have been life-long friendships, were no more. People dug into their positions and there were arguments, there was yelling; there were emotional breakdowns. After a few days, I told the judge, we will not be able to come to a consensus.

Of course, we had no idea how much the trial had affected the community. There were people mobbing the courthouse to offer their support. There were marches at the police station, protests, and vigils. The judge looked at me and said, "You need to come to a decision, one way or the other."

She sent us back, and she sent a court employee to

review the evidence. We watched the video from down the counter where you can see it's just a bottle, and that boy was clearly in the act of raising his hands. But I also know, that right arm's a little lower and his body's obscuring what he's doing. And as soon as that bottle clears him, the officer starts firing.

The worst of it is, I am incontrovertibly certain that boy was not the shooter. I believe he was terrified. I believed he panicked and was running for his life. And when he saw that woman step out her car, he saw an opportunity and took it. And, I have also been there.

I have known fear, I have known panic, and I have run for my life. I know the feeling of wanting to get away as fast as possible and as far as you possibly can. I believe that boy was running for his life – and then, it ended.

We watched that video, and one of the other jurors said, "You still think he's innocent?"

As I said, a lot of anger and hostility had arisen over those prior, several days. She asked, and then balled up a piece of paper and threw it at me.

I told her, "No. I don't think he's innocent." And, I shared, "I also don't think the officer is guilty."

And, I told them, I said, "I don't think the boy is guilty, either."

He was panicked, he fled, and none of what happened was thought through. But neither was it for the officer. They came to an active shooter scene, there was a woman pointing down the road, and screaming, "He took my car." That officer believed they were in pursuit of the shooter, and so he acted just like he was trained when peoples' lives are put in jeopardy.

This is a tragedy for everyone involved. And the one responsible, the one that started shooting – they are who's to blame. They are the reason all this happened, and they've never been held accountable. All those cameras, all those people, and no one and nothing can tell us who it was.

I was ready to throw in the towel, despite the wishes of the judge, except that balled up paper gave me an idea. So, I asked the judge for a cushion and a rock. She asked why, and I told her – for a demonstration – but I didn't tell her what. If I'd told her, I doubt that she'd have agreed: I went back and told the other jurors I could prove the officer wasn't guilty.

I told them I'd give them the cushion, and they'd have the opportunity of using it for defense, because the moment they walked into a room, I was going to either throw the rock at their heads, or that balled-up paper that woman threw at me.

The first one entered, and I wailed that rock at the wall beside them. I knew everybody heard, and she started cussing at me – she was angry: To think that I might really throw the rock at her. But you know what? She raised the cushion.

And so did every, last one of them. I told them, "All of you just shot that boy. You all thought I'd really throw the rock at you, so you raised the cushion to defend yourself. Even though – a lot of you didn't want to.

A week before that, any of us would have told you we had all grown close. By the time we delivered the verdict, I don't think any of us ever wanted to see another again. And it only kept getting worse.

The verdict was read, and you could hear that mother's heart breaking. There was only a brief moment of silence, and that woman let out the most heart-wrenching wail. Everything broke down, from there. Others joined her. There was shouting – anger. That court was unable to restore order. As we were being ushered out, we left to threats being leveled at us.

Can you blame them? They were there hoping to begin the process of healing, and instead we broke them worse.

So, this is where Remy found me – scrambled, I believe he said: And that is accurate.

Not long after that ended, several members of the jury made themselves available and blamed me for the decision. They said I forced their hand, and there were accusations that I was sympathetic to the man because of my military background. And, that is true. It gave me insight. And, I do hold sympathy for him, but just as much – moreso – for that child and his family. What happened is tragic for everyone, but blame and anger should be placed on the person that fired the weapon at the school.

But that didn't happen. Instead, I became the most hated man in the city, which led to protests at my home and practice.

At the condo, it was just irritating to fellow residents, though, I believe many sympathized. At the practice, however, it interrupted our ability to conduct business. A lot of cancellations started piling.

So, the other owners and I went to breakfast and they offered to purchase my fraction of the business. I told them I appreciated the offer, but I'd just walk. I went to collect my possessions, and as I enter, my receptionist says, "Someone left this." A bottle of bourbon.

Now, I've shared a lot with you. You've gained more insight than you really needed, however and because of that, you probably understand that I realized I had some things I needed to address.

For example, that mother's agony and sense of loss was recognized as the well that I'd carried with me for several decades. I realized I had never gotten over losing my parents. I realized it was affecting my ways in a manner that was not positive.

I was good when my hands were on something, but when there was time to reflect and examine my life, I understand, I did not render myself particularly well. It's why relationships have failed. And as I reflected, as I took a sip of bourbon that was unlike any I'd ever tried, I realized that when I'm in the field, when I'm with patients, I am doing something that brings appreciation. I am getting that affirmation that was missing in my early years. A hole in my being that was filled for fifteen years by my amazing parents.

So, that's whole lot of story, but I feel like it lets me shortcut here. I believe you'll understand when I tell you that what I'm doing here's the same: I find the fulfillment my soul needs in helping these people, and I take the trust they've given me with the highest degree of responsibility.

So – I do – appreciate what Remy's doing: I appreciate the conversation. But what you need to understand is in the end, Remy will do whatever he needs to protect his people. And so will I: I will do whatever it takes to protect these people.

So, I want to make this absolutely crystal clear – this is what I'm telling you: If you won't work with us as we will outline, I – will – be forced to kill you.

A proposition

It's my fault we've gotten here, already.

"It isn't, Remy. They are at fault for disregarding numerous warnings. They were told there would be consequences. They have no one to blame but themself."

Still – you know: I don't particularly care for this part of it. This was what my mother said I wasn't ready for, and I concede it: I hate it. But what Dr. Cohen says is also – that's on target: You had your warnings. You were told to stay away. We told you, if you cross the border another time, we would take action. You were told – explicitly told – that could mean you lose your life.

But you still came back.

You still snuck back and interfered while we were in the middle of an intervention. That – is unforgivable. You put all of us at risk, but more than anyone, you took the life of that child to the precipice of failure. So, that's where you've brought yourself. You have a choice to make, and from what I see, I don't think you're gonna like it. It's why my mother never gave one.

At least, not that I'm aware of.

"You are being given an opportunity. I know, this is not what you were looking for, but it's where you've brought yourself. Remy is pushing back against long-held traditions and significant opposition to give you a chance. I would recommend that you seriously consider taking it."

Like I told you, my mother has her opinions. When she was the first defense, there was no leniency, whatsoever: You violated our territory – it was a capital offense.

Quick, and unexpected. She says it minimized the suffering.

Well, I never liked it. I hate suffering. I hated watching our children wither. I hated seeing violators brought down. But seeing violators eliminated was not way I faced my mother.

That was only for the children.

That was the hope that we could find someone that we could trust to help our children, and we have been blessed with a person that could not be more capable. Dr. Cohen has demonstrated that the offer we gave him was duly rewarded. He has proven he will not only help our ailing children, but as much, he will stand with us and the others in the valley to protect our community. And while we have just begun to touch on what that is, I believe you understand that we are not like others you have encountered.

You understand that we are not like the other beings that live across this planet. You've heard the words Coal says, and you've heard the warnings shared by others.

What you didn't understand is that Coal is ignorant, and the others warned you for your benefit. But I want to share with you what Coal is not able to accept: He should be grateful.

Before I wore this role, my mother led this nation, and she led it like those before her determined was best for us. We pushed others from the valley, and struck down any that thought to test us. There's a long history and treaties that have been placed, but leave it to say – we were given the space we claimed. As more, and more moved across the country, documents were signed that confirmed our sovereignty, and that wasn't for our protection – it's for yours. We've been telling all of you to leave us alone since you crossed this valley. We tried leaving well enough alone when you moved in and started mining – we established an agreement. But then the road they used got paved and turned into a highway. And, more recently, that development over the ridge, and everything that followed.

You all have encroached upon us. You have probed, and questioned, and sent agents in, and all we ever wanted was to be left alone. But, for some reason. You all can't do that. You keep pushing: For information, and sometimes trying to take advantage. And that's where we come to Coal.

I won't pretend I don't dislike him. He's a fool that got a badge, and he thinks that elevates him beyond his evident stupidity. He is a crass moron that convinces other people to do things for which he doesn't have the courage, and I don't now – if that's you.

But what he doesn't understand is how lucky he is that he even exists, because my mother is not forgiving. However, she does hold a deep respect for the love you all hold for one another, and that's where Coal's story comes from: My mother has not always acted – the word, doctor.

"Unilaterally."

Alright: Like he said. She had her rules. She reacted like she did, and there was no room for excuses: You cross the line, you're fertilizer for the forest. But Coal's dad got one of her exceptions. And, that was not because of him – it was Coal's mother.

I believe Coal's family came into the area when the highway was being paved. I have no idea what role they had in all of that, but from what I've heard they were – again: Doctor, what's the word?

"Antagonistic."

Vile, is what I was searching for.

They came onto our land and meant to press their violence onto one of ours, and they quickly regretted that they did. They followed a woman back that had only shown them kindness and shared the Maker's gift. They followed her back to the territory they had been told was forbidden.

Back then, we didn't need to mark the region: There was no one here. You had the miners, but they were grateful for what we shared. And once they'd gone, there was nothing here for years.

The Hollers, of course. A few others.

The Hollers, you know, have been refining their recipes for hundreds of years – they've been here a long time. But that was mostly because no one else was and they wouldn't get bothered – being as close to us as they were.

But then, that highway. I don't know how you don't call that a violation of our agreement, but the governor argued the road was already here. He also agreed there'd be no more development in the valley – we gave him a little demonstration on why that would be a bad idea. He also contacted your federal government, and they agreed – it's a bad idea to bother us.

"Periodically, they have."

Sometimes… Sometimes they try to slip someone in, and I don't know if some of those working on the road were one of them, but there were seven that disregarded everything they'd been told.

Well, you don't need me to tell you: Violations are not taken lightly, and with their intent exposed, they were violently introduced to our capabilities.

Now, she didn't kill them. She roughed them up and mangled them pretty good, but she left them breathing, because that was another good example for the governor and others, of what happens when you interfere with us.

So, we made up a council. My mother oversaw the proceedings, and locals and government officials were invited to oversee.

I've heard it was a grand show. Each one of them was brought before the council, and none of them had a pinch of room to attempt any level of denial: They were guilty of violating our territory and the sentence for that is death. So, that's what they were given.

Now, those that were allowed to be present for those proceedings had been carefully selected. However, we hadn't been aware that one of those that were facing death had got involved with someone local.

I will tell you, there are some complicated relationships in this valley. But one complication we weren't prepared for was that the young woman that one young man had got involved with was a Holler. As difficult as it is to believe, Coal Slightman is a member of the Holler family.

Now, you're probably thinking – so, there are exceptions. And exceptions have been made, but there's got to be a real good argument. In this case, and like I've told you – my mother's got a soft spot for the relationships you people form. She let this Holler plead her case for love.

My mother is not cruel, but she is explicit: If you violate our territory, there is a terrible price to pay. But she was moved by the young woman. However, there was going to have to be a seal over any agreement to spare that man's life, so she agreed she would, so long as he lived in the valley. He also had to kill the other six.

Coal does not know about this. Coal believes we have slighted his family and kept them from success. In truth, Coal's father was a potential rapist and trespassed on our land. Both of those are capital crimes on the land on which you stand. I'll also point out, it's a capital crime for a citizen of your county to kill six others without reason.

But that's what Coal's father did, and now Coal grew up to be a sheriff.

So, they don't like us, but why they don't is because of what they've done. We only tried to be kind and considerate – just like we did with you, but here we are, again. Your offer's gonna be the same as theirs – without the killing someone.

You are hereby, formally invited into our territory. If you accept, you cannot leave this valley, and if you try, you will be executed: No exceptions. You can think about it, and you can talk to others that have made that choice, but those are your options.

You can stay here and live with us, or you will die. That is your choice – same one we gave the doctor.

"Remy."

The doctor's different – alright? That was the offer given, and he chose to die. That's when my mother stepped in.

"You came to me. I was not accepting an ultimatum. From my perspective, they had lured me down here under false pretense. If they wanted to kill someone that could help them, that was – their – choice."

He told us that, and he left. I was goin' after him, but mother stopped me. But that's a risk we took for someone special: You're no one. You're either an idiot that wouldn't listen, or someone sent you. Either way, you don't offer us anything.

"I was under the impression you were just another person. I had no understanding of who you were and knew nothing about the agreements with the federal government. I do not hold it against him, but there was some subterfuge. I also did not understand that your mother's invitation was meant to bind me here. You, on the other hand, are well aware you were not to have crossed the boundary. You were explicitly warned of the potential penalty. But you still chose to interfere, again."

Dr. Cohen: I was not trying to fool you. I'd decided you weren't the right one, and when mother asked for help, I told you: I said, don't. So, I don't feel that's being fair.

"Regardless, I was not told what I was potentially facing."

Your mother informed me there was a child that was ill and hoped I'd help. So, yes, you did tell me not to, but I thought I was looking at a typical, human child. My point is, I had no idea what I was getting into – and our friend, here, did. That's all I'm saying. I consider it an honor – in fact: I carry as my duty to help you in any way I can. I've told you, being a part of this community fills the void I've felt since my parents passed. And having our intervention nearly disrupted? That gets me as angry as anyone.

That's what you saw. When you crept upon us, we were trying to help an ailing child. You should feel extremely fortunate they've decided to extend the consideration that they have. Because what you saw cannot be shared with others. That is not the sole reason Sheriff Slightman's parents haven't shared what happened, but that's part of it.

His mother is a Holler, and his father has experienced what happens when you wrong these people. So, I would consider what they've offered. With the development of Grange, there's plenty here.

You will not be allowed to walk away with the knowledge that you've gained – and, I know there's great temptations. I know – I have been there. I have thought I could share everything and it could possibly lead to great revelations.

As I've told you, when Remy's mother invited me to the other side, I believed they needed me to help a child. And – I do believe – they found great amusement at my attempts.

"I have to listen for her heart beat."

Remy mocks.

I attempted to begin the examination as I would normally. I put my hand on her forehead and she felt cold. I asked her to open her mouth, but I could not get a good look in there. And then, I pulled out my stethoscope, to listen.

"Mother said, 'You won't need that.'"

She did. I tried to take the child's temperature, and she said the same thing. So I started to explain that's how it works.

"Mother said, 'No.'"

She said, no. And then, she did something that struck me very peculiar: She offered me a drink. She said, "This is all you'll need."

Again, I told you: Part of what got me down here was the bottle. I'd spent some time here and evenings almost always ended at the Hollers. So, I was familiar with the spirits. I had come to appreciate their qualities, and especially, the first one that got them started: Simply called, Holler's Spirit.

There's a secret about that particular spirit, and how I gained introduction to that was also unusual. Remy had walked in and asked how much for a sandwich? Like I always did – like everyone does – I looked over and offered my greeting.

Now, the question, itself, did not seem unusual. But then Rally asked, "How much you got?" And, he was told:

"Twenty four."

Remy told him, "That'll do."

Now, I can tell you, Remy was not looking for a sandwich. He was questioning the quantity that Rally needed. Twenty-four is a full casting: Remy was taking an order.

So, I'm sure, you wonder: What is it? What is the Maker's gift? The answer is, no one can tell you. It is quite precisely the Maker's gift. It comes from the earth on a regular basis, but only for certain people.

I'm sure you've guessed that Remy's one of them.

Anyway, I didn't know that's what she's offering. I thought it was just another spirit. But no: She gave me a straight shot of the Maker's gift, and, oh my Lord, I was immediately seeing the world differently – I was seeing a lot of what you saw, yesterday. But what took me into shock, what I never could have expected was that where that little girl was lying, was only lights.

Like a long string of warmly glowing Christmas lights, all jumbled together. That warm, glowing, golden white that I know you saw rising to the forest canopy. Rising like streams in distinct rows. And that's what I understood instantly: Everyone else that had stood around me, rose like neatly ordered lights – the girl was scrambled. What they were asking me to do was untangle the string of Christmas lights.

Of course, I had no clue. I meant to talk but it felt like I was suspended in a warm ocean. I could feel the presence of something within which I was held, but it was encompassing, and I wasn't able to put a form to it. I was clueless, and confused, but it was beautiful.

It was such a warm feeling, and everything that had weighed on my mind felt alleviated. The only thing that bothered me, were the scrambled lights. I had no idea what I should do, and no one's telling me, so, I did the only thing that I could think of: I tried untangling the lights.

And the funny thing about it is, that is in fact like sorting out a string of lights. That's exactly what's needed. Because, if we don't, those lights grow dim and the child withers.

That's what you interrupted, yesterday. You believed you went completely undetected and started documenting. You risked the life of a child, and that is unforgivable. I recommend you consider that while you determine if you want to join us – and it is us, now. I am not changed from who I was, but I do consider this my community, and if you choose to join us, I will protect you with every means at my disposal. And, if you choose not to – then, I protect them.

Final plea

I know it's not easy to consider giving up so much of what you've known. That's why I said, no. That's why I told them I'd rather be dead. The truth is, I still didn't have an understanding of who they were, and I thought, with my training, with my experience – I bet I could escape the clutches of these people. That's when Remy meant to kill me.

Everything was fading fast – I had no idea what was happening, but everything was dark, and I couldn't feel, nor hear anything.

There was a brief flicker before I heard, "Let him go." His mother let the light shine and called him off.

There's no escaping them, is what I'm telling you. Ten years ago, you would have been dead the moment they detected you. They would have interrupted the proceedings the instant you crossed the border. Remy's changed that – but it's only a degree. And if we weren't close as we were when you came upon us, they would have broken the intervention. It is quite possible that you could have caused the death of one of their children.

You are fortunate that Remy is comparatively young, and was not prepared for everything required of the role that he took on. It brought him to test out other ways – and his mother let him. She's tough as they come, but she also cares deeply about this community.

You are being given this opportunity, but it does – indeed it does – come with an unshakable tether. You step a foot beyond where you've been told you can – it will go dark, instantly.

I know: You're looking at my agreement and feel like it's unfair. That I'm privileged and got a better deal

– and, I did. But that's because they asked me here and I can help them. You've got nothing to offer them – nothing at all. It's also not like that tether doesn't travel with me.

I – can – go anywhere I want; anytime I want. But there will always be another with me. And that's not so much because of trust – I like to believe they trust me – but rather concern about agents, or some unscrupulous person that holds ideas. They're with me so that if something happens – everything goes dark.

My request to have them kill me is a standing order. If I am compromised, then, I give my life.

Now, I believe, that if over time you can demonstrate you are trustworthy, I do believe that they could extend the same to you. But there is going to be a process. No one else has yet been allowed that freedom, and – I do – consider it a privilege. I do understand the risk they've taken, so I choose my activity carefully, and with coordination.

I've gone back to the city on several occasions. I've shared time with those I've known. I've gone to Southeast Asia, and I've travelled several nations where I previously would not have felt welcome. There is a security to have someone with me, and I also accept if I am compromised, I do not want to imperil those in this community.

There are benefits, and there are compromises, and you will mostly be compromised for several years. But that does not mean you cannot continue living life. This is a wonderful community, and we have accepted the growing town, over the ridge. That town has at least a little of the familiar – theatre, stores, and there's always the distillery. Certainly, there are many that have claimed to hold freedom that have less. But I get it – I do.

None of that's convincing.

I could tell you they'll add years to your life, I could tell your being part of this community is tremendously fulfilling, and you'd still – either – say as I did, or plan subterfuge that isn't going to last a minute. I understand it, I get it, and I know our efforts are extraordinarily inadequate. But it is also the only card you have to continue living. Just as we said when we started talking, the last thing we want to do is bring you harm, but that was, and is your decision.

You've brought us here.

Remy's been unreasonably patient with those that are incapable of following the simplest instructions – myself included. He's created an opportunity to contribute, to learn, and to live. He is a kind person – he is not cruel. He does not want to hurt anyone or anything, but he has also grown into his role and will do whatever he has to do to protect his people. He has come to understand – he is the front line. He is the face and first defender of these people.

So am I, in case you needed a reminder. Remy's the face, but I am his soldier. All my training and experience will be used at his bequest. I am human, but I am one of the people. The secrets and missions held to chest, the loyalty to my country and willingness to die for it, are now transferred to where I stand: These – are my people. However, I – like Remy – I hope you will consider you can find a place here.

I hope you can understand that what we've offered is not cruel. It's not limiting. If you are an agent of the government – if you have family: There are ways we can work with you. We can make arrangements for what you've known to be incorporated. This is not everything being taken away – it is a new beginning. We just need you to understand, your commitment, going forward, has to be to – us.

Now, let me give you a second to reflect. I know we've come at you, these past few days, and we've shared a lot, offered information, and also, not said a lot. I believe Remy intends to go down that road, but I want you to know that what we're doing's a work in progress.

As we told you, there've been a few that have joined us.

There have also been some that didn't want to.

We're trying to make it clear that there really isn't a choice: You meet our terms, or the response is what it always has been. Remy's just been trying to make this a gentler introduction. Unfortunately, from what we've seen, those that are willing don't take this long to make a decision.

And I – I will tell you: I'm disappointed.

I don't know who you are, nor anything about you, but we want to. We want to hear where you're from, who you care for, what ambitions you might hold, and what your reasons were for disregarding all our warnings. We've shared with you, and I hope you will share the same with us. We want you to see this not as punishment, but an opportunity that few that have crossed the line have gotten. We don't care if you're an agent of the government, or just a victim of poor judgment and curiosity. But your days are numbered for letting Remy know if you'll accept his proposition. It's a window – not a standing offer.

And, I – I know: I've gone on about this more times than you wanted to hear, but being part of this community has healed me. What was missing when I was young, that missing part of what I needed that was filled by family – my parents – I've found that, here. I never thought I'd feel complete again, and while I've spent much of my life unaware it was needed, I now understand I need to feel like I am contributing. I need to feel like I am valuable to my community and those I care about. And that's – you know – I look back:

When I lost my parents, I was engaged to be married. And, it's not only her fault. I was young, I felt successful, and I had support from my family. But it was probably a relationship that was always doomed to fail, because I didn't realize what I needed. She saw me as a young, successful – potential – doctor, and I saw her as a beautiful woman that loved living life. But neither of those is the basis for a sustained relationship – not one that isn't forced. Neither of us appreciated each other for who we are. As a person. For what we offer, as a being, to support the spirit of another.

That's something I lost when my parents were killed. That is something I didn't account for as I moved through one relationship after another – and it only got worse as the years wore on. By the time I came down here, I'd mostly sworn relationships off, especially young women – sometimes young men – that demonstrated interest. I understood what they were looking for, and though I couldn't put it into words, I knew that wasn't what I needed.

I knew what I longed for was the family that I'd lost. People that were – there – for one another.

And I'm – I know: I go on about it. But I cannot stress the difference it makes to have parents like that. Coming from where I came from, desperate for something I didn't understand, I moved into a home where they would listen. I – knew – they cared about me. Not dollars in an account. Not a title. Not what I could do: They cared about me. Even when I was a pain in the ass – and I knew it then.

It wasn't always easy – I'm not claiming that. The first years, especially: I was a wild-child from the forest. I pushed back, clawed back, and refused to join with the programs of society: My parents never put a finger on me, but they did – they surely did – demand discipline. And that demand started with their own – listening, and responding. Even when what I said was petulant. Even when the words I'd spit at them were irrational and thoughtless. But they still listened. They responded without a hint of anger. I don't know if I would have had that same patience – especially after losing them – however, by the time I got to high school, I wasn't looking to rebel, I was looking to make them proud.

They were two of the most patient people that have ever lived, and I can tell you that by the time I lost them, they had appreciation for what I contributed to our relationship – as much – as I had for them.

We knew it, because we shared it. And that's not something I had or realized until I started working here.

I've found that here.

I realized it: What I'd been missing. It was my failing as much as any other. And that was an epiphany. It hit me after Remy came to ask some questions – still sorting how he wanted to move with things. But he apologized for bothering me, and then he thanked me for the information.

I realized, this young – probably not as young as we imagine – but he's inexperienced, regardless. And he's coming, looking for insight, looking for input – from me. He valued my opinion.

It was a striking moment for me. Here's this young man that's got me by – you know: I'm at their mercy. He comes to me, and he's trusting what I answer. He engaged me with the sort of conversation that I'd only held with parents: Naked honesty with no shadows of duplicity nor feints.

I've come to think very highly of him – I consider him a friend – and he is only one of many. I guess – you know... This is – you might find this amusing.

It wasn't long after I had this idea arrive that what was failing in my life was failing to truly connect with others. As I began to interact more honestly, I began to feel pretty high and mighty. I began to consider what this opportunity truly meant for me. And, as part of considering these thoughts, I decided to visit Annie.

You know, there's all sorts of conversations, and clouds, ideas, and uncertainty with her, but she'd only ever been friendly. So, I got the idea I'd ask her to join me for a drink. You know what she said?

That's right: Not with that nasty child from her youth and memory.

I still haven't won that battle.

She also said, her and Rally, but you wouldn't know that, even if you kept them underneath a microscope.

I suppose – not funny. I thought it was an amusing anecdote, and there was an idea behind it: Your life's not over. You may be limited in your travels, but there is a lot of life to live for, here.

There is a lot to do here.

You may not find connections as strongly, nor securely as I find I have. You may not be able to contribute as fully as I can. But you can find connections, and you can contribute. There's a lot that goes on in this valley, and you'll have access to some things you never would have.

I want you to understand, this – can – be a good thing.

I don't know how many more days Remy will let you have, but it's not many. There's a lot more than just sitting in a forest, and you're not required to. You can have a home. You can have a family. You can still pursue some sort of career if you so choose. But, you're going to have to decide what you want to do.

If you have any questions, or, you want to talk, I'll be down at Rally's.

Vivication

You're nervous.

That's probably a sign you're thinking about things that are not going to happen. I've given you an opportunity and – I'm telling you – that's what you should do. But I know, I already know you expect some sort of contingency. I know that because I've been dealing with your contingency.

I've got Remington taking in reports all over the valley. I've got one that's been sneakin' around the edges tryin' to size up the best place to make his run. And, I've warned that man: You try it – you'll end up where your partner's gone. So, I see what's going on. I know what you think is gonna happen, but now that I know you're a federal agent, I also know you're worried that some of what you read might not be fabricated. So, you're thinkin', like everybody thinks: Where's their weakness?

That's the origin of your ill-advised adventure. You read about our people. You see reports and read agreements – those are for your benefit. We don't need agreements to protect ourselves – we've got our maker. And we've been generously sharing our Maker's gift since you all first trespassed across our valley.

But you don't care, do you? You have to come down here and poke around. You've got an undying curiosity and need to understand what – you-are-not-able.

So, I'll put it to you simple: There is nothing you can do to understand us. You will never infiltrate us, or whatever it is that you intend. And you will also – never – be able to use the good doctor for your purposes, nor against us. Because he is one of us. He has become a member of our community. And this community is impervious – to you.

I don't know if you consider yourself an atheist. I don't know if you believe a powerful God stands behind you. I don't know, and it doesn't matter, just like it didn't matter in the past – all those times you've seen an unfortunate decision documented: Those are events that occurred that should not be replicated. Those agreements are not suggestions. They are warnings to protect you. Because if you attempt to violate our community, you will not be facing us. You will face our Maker. And when you do, you will find you stand alone, with no God there to protect you.

There is no one coming for you.

That's not a threat. I'm just trying to make it clear: Your options are what I've given you.

There is no God, and there is no operation to extract you: You are alone, and the time for you to answer ends at sundown.

Now, I know Dr. Cohen has continued talking to you. I know he's tried to explain that joining our community has advantages. I know he told you there are certain freedoms that he's retained, and he told me, he said, you might, some day.

You won't. You will live in the valley, and that is it. Dr. Cohen is not bound by the same restrictions, because Dr. Cohen is different. We told you that. And, in case it wasn't already completely clear, we are also different.

We do not have the same origins as the humans on this planet. Whether you want to believe in Adam and Eve, or you find evidence for evolution – neither is the origin of my people. That's what you came here for – am I right?

You want to know who we are; what we are. You wanted to know our capabilities and where we came from. You believe because we're different we are a threat, and you want to know our ambitions.

Well, I'll tell you: Our ambitions are to fulfill the wishes of our Maker. We were told, this is where we will live and we are responsible for caring for everything in this valley. I imagine this is hard for you to comprehend, but that is our sole purpose. That is the only ambition that we carry, and for the first people that came through here, that did not strike them as unusual, nor outrageous. They understood and shared many of the same traditions. Before the European settlers arrived, there were no restrictions. We lived together and the Maker's gift was incorporated into some cultures.

Now, we knew we were different. We knew we had different origins, and they didn't have the lights. But we got along fine, most of the time. And that's what's led to most of our problems.

When the Europeans followed through, they brought a whole different set of ideas, and the first mistake we made was letting them walk into the valley unencumbered. We let them build their mine, and we allowed the road to scar our valley. This was a mistake that was against the Maker's desires, and our interactions became increasingly antagonistic.

So we moved them out. We shut down the mine and told them, this is our land and you are no longer welcome.

Now, all of this is very recently – only hundreds of years. Our experience with the other people had lasted thousands. So, you understand, we'd been conditioned. We did not understand the differences you claim. We thought the explanation of our Maker's gift would be completely adequate.

That misunderstanding led to the first time people tried to breach the borders of our land, and that's where we got our very first agreement: Keep out of here, and we won't bother you. Based upon the experiences that were documented, that worked out pretty well, for a while.

But then, it was decided that the road that was partly cut from when the mine was here, would be a good way to connect different regions. This was during a period where the person prior to my mother was representing, and I believe my mother would have pushed back much more harshly. But it was agreed. And, at that time, there was nothing for anyone to stop at. The only people we interacted with were a random few out hiking, or those that met difficulty, passing through. Then, that development got started up on the ridge.

Now, my mother's watching this. You know my mother: She does not waste words. She had what they started disassembled, and the equipment was broken down to the smallest parts. This brought the more recent problems that we've experienced.

Sheriffs and state police came to investigate, and they walked onto our territory as if they had the right. As they did not walk off, a larger investigation ensued, at which point prior agreements were once again enforced.

I do want to point out, my mother was uncharacteristically conciliatory. This valley is ours, but there were several that had lived here for a considerable time, and we had no problem with them - notably, the Hollers across the river. So, my mother said, we'll let people in the valley, so long as they respect it. The exception is the area that's bordered by the highway, the creek coming down the hill, the ridge, and where the valley ends. That area's well-posted. Despite that, people still seem to have a hard time respecting our territory.

The whole valley's ours, in case I wasn't clear. We can close it down, if we so desire. The law of the land within this valley – is ours. When you and yours arrived conducting governmental business, you were already in violation of our agreements.

Of course, that wasn't clear at first. We didn't know who you were. Once we realized – I will tell you: I did begin to anger. I was extremely frustrated, because this is exactly what mother warned.

She told me this would happen.

She said, if we bring another in, they will see him as a conduit. They will see him as a way to gather information. A way to find out what we are in hopes of using the Maker's powers.

Yes – I was angry, because here you were. And then, we start to realize there are others. And, at that point, I figured I should have listened to my mother. At that point, I went and got her because I felt like I was moving into trouble. I told my mother, "I believe I have made a terrible mistake.

And, do you know what my mother said? She said, "No. You didn't." She shook my suggestion off and she smiled. Because she absolutely loves having Dr. Cohen with us.

For the children, of course. But also, because Dr. Cohen's a good person. He helps with every aspect of our community – including – talking with you.

We didn't ask him.

He just wants to.

So, I'm at a state where I had a lot of doubts. I had conflicting feelings – I knew I was getting scrambled. So, I asked my mother, "What should I do?" And, she told me, "That's a question for our Maker."

Now, I have never spoken directly with our Maker. I have felt the Maker's presence when we go into the veil, and I feel the Maker's touch everywhere I am, but I would never have considered my trivial distractions worthy of address. But my mother said to.

So, I climbed on top of Chantry rock from which the spring spills free to feed the Maker's gift. I let the light flow free and questioned if I had done the right thing.

Now, when we enter into the veil there is a sense of peace, and warmth, and comfort. However, I have never felt an intensity of those so great as in our Maker's presence. And our Maker told me, "You are on the right path."

Can you believe that? I have been given the word of our Maker that I have done the right thing. I was so excited that I jumped down and meant to tell my mother, but then – I remembered you.

So, that's why I haven't been around. I had to talk to the rest of those that were poking around. I went down to Rally's, and there were four.

I explained, their presence in the valley conducting business for your country was already in violation. I pointed out, that already meets the criteria for a capital sentence. And, I suggested to them, they should leave as soon as possible. I told them, they still had that opportunity but my patience was running out. I told them, you will not be leaving with them.

So, there's no one coming for you. Any plan they

had has been abandoned. You — are abandoned: There's no one coming to your rescue.

You see, everyone says were something: Vampires, aliens; sometimes just monsters. But we aren't that. We don't describe ourselves as anything but ourselves. Put here by our Maker, to live here and care for the magic in this valley. Some people also look at us like we're one of them, and that's an unfortunate mistake one of your friends made.

He put his hands on me.

This was at Rally's, and unfortunately there's tourists, but you understand: He was incinerated instantly. There was nothing left but a little bit of ash that floated to the floor.

I tried to sound intimidating to the three that's left. I said, "Don't make the same mistake." I told them, "That's two you're down. There's no need for any more." I told them, "Respect the agreements that we have."

Diplomatic outreach arrived shortly after.

So that's it. What you came for: We were put here by our Maker. We are a conduit as needed to protect what's ours. But that power is the Maker's and we do not ask for it, nor access it. We only do what our Maker's asked of us, and that's — take care of everything you see around us.

That's everything. There's nothing else to know. As far as we know we've been here forever, and we plan to continue staying here forever.

I'll come back after the sun goes down, but that's the last time. You've had enough time to come to a decision.

The stranger

Streams of lights rise into the quiet dark of the evening sky. Golden orbs float with neat, consistent spacing in endless trails that leave the whole hillside bathed warmly and aglow. They appear translucent, but nothing can be seen through the other side, even nights when the full moon brushes them in silver light.

The air remains warm, and there is already dew that clings to leaves and grasses. The night is comfortable and encompassing. A gentle breeze wafts amongst the trills of insects and erratic outbreaks from forest creatures. There is otherwise no sound, outside of the occasional vehicle that passes along the unlit highway.

"Remy," weeps the curtain across the music of the evening. It brings a lanky figure digging footsteps in the hillside to break from peace and solitude, with, "Remy."

The doctor calls, "Remy: Wait for me."

One is breathing heavily as they meet. It is unclear if the other even breathes. They join together and the doctor questions, "This is it?"

The answer holds disappointment: "I think his decision's been made. Probably always has been."

"Any chance?"

There is greater disappointment, still, as Remy answers, "No," because, "I don't know if he still thinks they're coming, or if he thinks he can make a break, or maybe – maybe, after everything he's seen, after everything we've told him – maybe he thinks all of this is fake. Maybe he just doesn't believe anything we've told him."

"We tried," is offered as reassurance, but it doesn't.

"We tell them everything. They come looking for answers, looking for weapons; looking for understanding. And once we give all of it to them, everything they had questions of, and ideas that they'd formed, suddenly – they disregard it all. The first couple days I thought we might've had him, but after that…"

"There is nothing more that you could have done. You have been exceedingly patient."

"I know, doc, but everything that happened is exactly like my mother said. She's right about everything."

"And your Maker," it's reminded: "Told you to continue what you're doing."

"Yeah," is agreed, however, "Please don't use our Maker's name. No offense, Doctor Cohen."

"I'm not offended. However, I do not feel it is a transgression. If your Maker tells you otherwise, I will duly respect that request. Otherwise, I feel it's reasonable to refer to this entity in conversation. Share your thoughts if you disagree."

"It's not that. I just worry about something happening. You're just there, and it happens, and there's no warning."

"I heard," the doctor shares: Efforts made to cover up an incident allow enough to float a conversation. Something happened, even if the what is far from clear. An unfortunate incident that was likely to have been completely necessary. Still, "I know you don't like seeing that."

"There were tourist," Remy says while trying to temper the distaste: "In front of everyone. The Maker's gift should help them forget, but it seems like a risk we shouldn't take."

"I think – your Maker – understood they were trying to do something that would be harmful to you. I believe that action was taken as an absolute necessity to protect someone that's viewed as eminently capable of leading their people though rapidly evolving circumstances. I – also – see that in you, and I – also – stand beside you. I will also do anything required to protect you."

"I know – I know. Let's get this over with."

The pace is brought down with the doctor present. Feet no longer dig into the earth to move the body quickly, and the two leisurely climb through the streaming lights and towards a person that's been confined within them for several days.

Arrival is met with continued silence. Not a word has been spoken back and there's been little tell and almost no reaction – no matter what's told; no matter the demonstration.

They remain seated in a chair that is faultlessly comfortable. They watch as two approach but show the same disinterest they have from the beginning. The same disinterest demonstrated on initial warning. The same lack of concern shown when consequence was shared. But their eyes do dart momentarily, as the lights that have surrounded them begin to dissipate.

It is the first time, in days, there's been a sense of tension – Remy says, "I hope you'll join us."

"Sincerely," the doctor adds: "We want you to

accept our invitation. We will help you find a way to make the experience rewarding. Please accept the offer, like Remy says: We want you to be a part of what we're doing."

For the first time, the man speaks. There is no fear in his voice – it is almost sinister. It is as if a certainty is still held that plans will be enacted. As if flaunting his position, the man asks, "You don't have any questions about who I am?"

To this, Remy answers, "We know." And, furthermore, "We told you that." It is made patently clear, "They aren't coming. I hope you don't still believe they're coming for you. Because what we gave you is the only option that you have."

The man says, "Remington Bowlin. There's nothing you want to know?"

A trigger's pulled that is foretelling of what will follow. There is a ring to the voice that brings the doctor to know, "You're doctor Schumann."

The revelation is the distraction that is wanted: With well-honed agility, a quick twist leaves the chair, and feet dig for the summit escape. Well-rested legs move quickly until the lights begin to rise, but the ridge is near, and they have just begun. They cannot stop the progress as Remy pleads, desperately – he shouts, "Don't run."

A brief glance back watches as a pistol's drawn, and the doctor warns, "Stop – or I shoot."

There is no reaction to the warning: Feet dig against the earth with desperation to get away. Panic and adrenaline fuel the run. There is daylight over the crest as the acme's neared, and relief pours cold sweat over the body, still certain reinforcement will be waiting.

That faith is shattered by the crack that echoes

across the valley, as a shot is fired and the final threads of evening peace are sheared away by the cry that follows. The sound of agony leaves the solitude of the valley rent and battered, a violence that echoes between the valley walls just like the fired bullet that traveled up the hillside to find its mark, that struck the stranger squarely in the back and saw him fall, face down against the earth.

"Doctor," holds only dismay.

There is no consideration for older legs as the other moves quickly towards the interloper. As the doctor arrives, the other is offering their salve.

"I can end it," the doctor suggests, but Remy offers, "No." He looks up – there is pain across his brow; sorrow in him – he says, "I'll send him gently."

Arms wrap a warm embrace that brings comfort, that is soothing, and all that can be seen are lights rising: Small, glowing orbs that rise, one after the other. The memory of violence and pain slip with them, with the gently spoken words:

You're safe, now. There's nothing to fight for. There's nothing else you need to do. Lean back and feel the warmth and comfort. Feel the warm embrace that's supporting you.

You're safe; you are protected.

You should see the lights – lights rising towards the heavens. Keep your eyes on them. Look into the light and let your body drift in that direction – stay focused on the light. Feel the warmth – feel the comfort.

You are safe. You are protected. There is nothing else to fight for.

Go into the light – let it wrap you. Let the light wash everything away.

"I think he's gone."

Shh, is uttered as fingers gently pull the eyelids closed, and a final offering is given:

Suffer the light to imbue thy mind and frame,
Suffer solace to fulfill you.
Let our Maker be thy guiding star,
And feel the glory ana thru.

Nye burden, nor jury on thy shoulder rests,
Taketh freely our light of mercy
Receive the Maker's gift, and forevermore,
Rest peacefully.

"Find peace, stranger."

There are only lights that feel as if they are flowing through the body. They grow brighter and flare into stunning brilliance with the final words, "Rest peacefully."